I FUNNY
SCHOOL OF LAUGHS

THE
MIDDLE
SCHOOL
SERIES

THE WORST YEARS OF MY LIFE
(with Chris Tebbetts)

This is the insane story of my first year at middle school, when I, Rafe Khatchadorian, took on a real-life bear (sort of), sold my soul to the school bully, and fell for the most popular girl in school. Come join me, if you dare...

GET ME OUT OF HERE!
(with Chris Tebbetts)

We've moved to the big city, where I'm going to a super-fancy art school. The first project is to create something based on our exciting lives. But I have a BIG problem: my life is TOTALLY BORING. It's time for Operation Get a Life.

MY BROTHER IS A BIG, FAT LIAR
(with Lisa Papademetriou)

So you've heard all about my big brother, Rafe, and now it's time to set the record straight. I'm NOTHING like my brother. (Almost) EVERYTHING he says is a Big, Fat Lie. And my book is 100 times better than Rafe's. I'm Georgia, and it's time for some payback... Khatchadorian style.

HOW I SURVIVED BULLIES, BROCCOLI, AND SNAKE HILL
(with Chris Tebbetts)

I'm excited for a fun summer at camp—until I find out it's a summer *school* camp. There's no fun and games here, I have a bunk mate called Booger Eater (it's pretty self-explanatory), and we're up against the kids from the "Cool Cabin"... there's gonna be a whole lotta trouble!

ULTIMATE SHOWDOWN
(with Julia Bergen)

Who would have thought that we—Rafe and Georgia— would ever agree on anything? That's right—we're writing a book together. Discover: Who has the best advice on BULLIES? Who's got all the right DANCE MOVES? Who's the cleverest Khatchadorian in town? And the best part? We want you to be part of the fun too!

SAVE RAFE!
(with Chris Tebbetts)

I'm in worse trouble than ever! I need to survive a gut-bustingly impossible outdoor excursion so I can return to school next year. Watch me as I become "buddies" with the scariest girl on the planet, raft down the rapids on a deadly river, and ultimately learn the most important lesson of my life.

JUST MY ROTTEN LUCK
(with Chris Tebbetts)

I'm heading back to the place it all began: Hills Village Middle School, but only if I take "special" classes... If that wasn't bad enough, when I somehow land a place on the school football team, I find myself playing alongside none other than the biggest bully in school, Miller the Killer!

DOG'S BEST FRIEND

(with Chris Tebbetts)

It's a dog-eat-dog world. When I start my own dog-walking empire, I didn't think it could go so horribly wrong! Somehow, I always seem to end up in deep doo-doo…

The
I FUNNY
Series

I FUNNY

(with Chris Grabenstein)

Join Jamie Grimm at middle school where he's on an unforgettable mission to win the Planet's Funniest Kid Comic Contest. Dealing with the school bully (who he also happens to live with) and coping with a disability are no trouble for Jamie when he has laughter on his side.

I EVEN FUNNIER

(with Chris Grabenstein)

Jamie's one step closer to achieving his dream! This time, be amazed as he fends off the attention of thousands of star-struck girls, watch in awe as he reduces the school bully to a quivering mess, and join the masses as he becomes the most popular kid in school.
Or something like that…

I TOTALLY FUNNIEST

(with Chris Grabenstein)

Jamie's heading to Hollywood for his biggest challenge yet. There's only the small matter of the national finals and eight other laugh-a-minute competitors between him and the trophy—oh, and a hurricane!

I FUNNY TV
(with Chris Grabenstein)
Jamie has achieved his dream of becoming the Planet's
Funniest Kid Comic, and now the sky's the limit! Enter a
couple of TV executives with an offer for Jamie to star
in his very own show…

THE
TREASURE HUNTERS
SERIES

TREASURE HUNTERS
(with Chris Grabenstein)
The Kidds are not your normal family, traveling the world
on crazy adventures to recover lost treasure. But when their
parents disappear, Bick and his brothers and sisters are
thrown into the biggest (and most dangerous) treasure hunt
of their lives. Evil pirates, tough guys and gangsters stand in
their way, but can they work together to find
mom and dad?

DANGER DOWN THE NILE
(with Chris Grabenstein)
Bick, Beck, Storm and Tommy are navigating their way
down the Nile, from a hot and dusty Cairo to deep dark
jungles, past some seriously bad guys along the way.

SECRET OF THE FORBIDDEN CITY
(with Chris Grabenstein)
The Kidds are desperately trying to secure the ancient
Chinese artefact that will buy their mother's freedom from
kidnapping pirates.

PERIL AT THE TOP OF THE WORLD

(with Chris Grabenstein)

When the biggest heist in history takes place in Moscow, the
Kidds rush in to save the day—but instead, they're accused of
being the thieves themselves!

HOUSE OF ROBOTS

(with Chris Grabenstein)

Sammy is just your average kid… except he lives in a
house full of robots! Most of the time it's pretty cool. But then
there's E, the worst robot ever. He's a know-it-all, thinks he's
Sammy's brother, AND he's about to go to the same school!
Come see if Sammy *ever* manages to make any friends with
a loser robot tagging along…

ROBOTS GO WILD!

(with Chris Grabenstein)

Sammy and E are finally making some friends at school.
But disaster strikes when E malfunctions just in time to be
upstaged by the super-cool new robot on the block.

ROBOT REVOLUTION

(with Chris Grabenstein)

When Sammy's inventor mom becomes distracted by a
top-secret project, the robots soon begin to fall into disrepair.
Cue a robot revolution!

KENNY WRIGHT SUPERHERO

(with Chris Tebbetts)
Kenny is the life-saving, world-famous superhero otherwise known as Stainlezz Steel. He's taken down General Zod twice, beaten Darth Vader at chess… and lives with his grandma. Ok, sometimes he gets a bit carried away. But G-ma really does need his help now—and he's going to have to be a superhero to save the day.

JACKY HA-HA

(with Chris Grabenstein)
With her irresistable urge to tell a joke in every situation—even when she really shouldn't—twelve-year-old Jacky Ha-Ha loves to make people laugh. And cracking wise helps distract her from thinking about not-so-funny things in her life, like her mom serving in a dangerous, faraway war, and a dad who's hardly ever home.

WORD of MOUSE

(with Chris Grabenstein)
Raised in a laboratory, Isaiah is extremely smart, but
scared of everything. One day, he manages to escape and
is forced to leave his family behind. All alone now, Isaiah
has to quickly learn to survive in the outside world. When
he meets a girl who is as unusual as he is, Isaiah soon sees
that even someone as small and as frightened as he is can
have the power to change the world.

I FUNNY
SCHOOL OF LAUGHS

JAMES PATTERSON
AND CHRIS GRABENSTEIN
With Emily Raymond
Illustrated by Jomike Tejido

1 3 5 7 9 10 8 6 4 2

Young Arrow
20 Vauxhall Bridge Road
London SW1V 2SA

Young Arrow is part of the Penguin Random House group of companies
whose addresses can be found at global.penguinrandomhouse.com

Penguin
Random House
UK

First published by Young Arrow in 2017

www.penguin.co.uk

A CIP catalogue record for this book is available from the British Library

HB ISBN 9781784754006
TPB ISBN 9781784754013

Printed and bound by Clays Ltd, St Ives Plc

Penguin Random House is committed to a sustainable future
for our business, our readers and our planet. This book is made from
Forest Stewardship Council® certified paper.

I FUNNY
SCHOOL OF LAUGHS

Chapter 1

DEAD MAN ROLLING

Hi, everybody, I'm Jamie Grimm and here are a couple of things you should know about me right away, since these will probably be my last days on Earth.

One, I'm a comedian.

Two, my cousin Stevie Kosgrov is going to kill me this coming Friday night at eight o'clock Eastern (seven o'clock Central).

Yep. I'm like a carton of milk. I have an expiration date. Because Friday nights at eight is when my new TV show, *Jamie Funnie,* airs on BNC-TV.

And, this time, Stevie might actually have a pretty good reason to destroy me. You see, just for yuks, we're shooting an episode making fun of Long

Beach Middle School's longest-running bully. We're halfway through the first season of *Jamie Funnie,* which tapes in New York, and guess what? My sitcom is a huge hit. Almost as big as the fist Stevie Kosgrov is going to hit me with when he sees this Friday's episode about Skeevy Musgrove! Guess we should've disguised his name better, huh?

My good friend Gilda Gold is directing the Skeevy episode. Our best buds Joey Gaynor and Jimmy Pierce are playing my best buds Joey and Jimmy. Yeah. The TV show is kind of based on my life. It makes things easier.

And much more dangerous.

"Quiet on the set!" calls Gilda. "Aaaaaand, *action!*"

We start the scene.

"Congratulations, Jamie," says Gaynor, sitting in the front row. "You won the Teacher for a Day Contest!"

Turns out, Gaynor is actually a pretty decent actor—way better than me.

Jimmy Pierce? Well, he's a brainiac. He more or less mumbles most of his lines.

"Yeah, Jamie," Pierce mumbles. "Congratulations,

man." (Actually, it sounds more like, "Yuh, Mamie. Math calculations, ham," which is sort of funny, so Gilda doesn't call "Cut" and the scene keeps going.)

"Class," I say, popping a wheelie, "as teacher for the day, I hereby outlaw homework for the rest of the year!"

"Whoa!" says Gaynor, totally in character. "Can you do that?"

"Today I am a teacher. Today I can do anything!"

"Even if it's about tomorrow?" asks the actress playing Jillda Jewel, who's sort of my love interest on the show (not that I have all that much interest in the mushy junk the writers keep coming up with). And, yes, she's kind-of-sort-of based on Gilda Gold.

"Teachers are like Roman emperors," I say.

"You mean they're all dead?" snarls the burly kid playing Skeevy Musgrove. "Just like you!"

Gilda gives the Skeevy actor a cue to raise his gigantic peashooter, which is about the size of an Amazonian blowgun.

"It's time to play dodgeball with spitballs!" he shouts as the prop guys use an off-camera air cannon to blast wet paper wads at me.

I duck, dart, dodge, rock, and roll to avoid all the

incoming projectiles. They splat on the wall behind me and sort of ooze their way down. It's gross, which means it's funny.

Skeevy goes to reload.

"As teacher for the day," I say as fast as I can, "I hereby declare that it's time for dessert!"

All the kids on the set pop open their lunch boxes and pull out cream pies. Then everyone hurls them at Skeevy!

He is *creamed*. By eighteen different pies, all of them made out of 100 percent whipped cream. Gloppy, foamy goop covers his head and dribbles down to plop into his lap. He looks like a whipped-cream abominable snowman.

"And that, class," I pronounce, "is another way to silence a bully. Fill his piehole with pie!"

Chapter 2

THAT'S NOT A SANDWICH, THAT'S A WRAP!

Okay, everybody," says Gilda. "That's a cut and a wrap. Episode number eleven is in the can! We'll edit it, sweeten the sound track, and air it on Friday. After that, *Jamie Funnie* is officially on a five-week hiatus!"

The studio audience cheers. The cast and crew cheer, too. We've been working pretty hard on the show for three months straight. Now we all get to take a well-earned vacation. Instead of being tutored on the set, next week Gilda, Gaynor, Pierce, and I will be heading back to Long Beach Middle School, where the real Skeevy Musgrove still reigns supreme. But these days, Stevie Kosgrov shares his head bully duties with Lars Johannsen, an eighth-grade giant who moved to Long Island from Minnesota. Lars is so big, I think he used to be Minneapolis.

It'll be weird going back to a real middle school instead of the fake one on the *Jamie Funnie* set. But I'm kind of looking forward to it. Middle school is where I've always found my best material. It's also where I first ate mystery meat, had my head stuffed into a toilet, and learned that there are three kinds of people in this world: those who are good at math and those who aren't. But, hey, it all turned into pretty good punch lines.

Life has really changed for my friends Gaynor, Pierce, and Gilda, too.

Gaynor has earned enough money to help out his mom, who is still recuperating from a bout with cancer. He's also bought himself a couple of new nose studs. One sparkles so much, it looks like an electronic zit.

Pierce, our resident genius, is saving his *Jamie Funnie* paychecks to bankroll his college education. At Harvard. *And* MIT. He wants to go to both at the same time.

"They are, actually, quite close to each other," he tells me. "I, of course, may need to purchase a hoverboard for the commute between campuses.

Or a drone. I need to crunch some numbers to determine which one would be most efficient."

Gilda? Well, she's already won a full scholarship to study filmmaking at UCLA. She's going to use the money she's made directing episodes of *Jamie Funnie* to finance her first independent feature film.

As for me, I'm putting away a big chunk of money in what I call my Medical Miracle Fund. I've gotten pretty good with my wheelchair, but who knows? Maybe someday there will actually be a cure for what ails the bottom half of me. Maybe aliens will land and their doctors will have a way to zap my spinal cord to make it work again. If they do, I want to be financially ready, just in case alien doctors don't accept most forms of major medical insurance.

I'm also doing everything I can to help my uncle Frankie keep his diner running, because, well, he always does everything he can to help me. I even offered to buy him a new jukebox. A deluxe digital-music dealio, with flashing LEDs and surround-sound speakers, that can stream the latest radio hits.

"Thanks but no thanks, kiddo," Uncle Frankie told me. "I only like vinyl doo-wop records. Doo-wop is like rap. But with a melody. And lyrics. And music. And harmonies. And…"

Yep. Uncle Frankie hates rap. "You can't yo-yo to it," he says.

I've also been helping out at Smileyville, which is what I call my aunt and uncle Smiley's house. That's where I live. In the garage. Actually, it's more like my personal Jamie cave, with remote-control gliding doors, a jumbo flat-screen TV, my red Mustang

11

convertible roommate, a fridge and microwave
for late-night nachos or s'mores, and all kinds of
gardening gear. Need a weed whacked? I'm your guy.

Smiley isn't my aunt and uncle's real last name.
I just call them that because they seldom smile.
They're missing the grin and chuckle genes, too.

Their real name is Kosgrov.

As in *Stevie* Kosgrov.

Yep. Long Beach Middle School's meanest bully
is their son, making him my cousin.

Which will make it super easy for him to cream
me on Friday night when his character gets
creamed on *Jamie Funnie*!

PIE-IN-THE-SKY IDEAS

Since I can't stop the earth's rotation (hey, I can't even walk), Friday night rolls around right on schedule.

We order pizza for dinner, which means I have to answer the door because the pizza delivery guy, Tony, is a budding stand-up comic. He likes to try out his jokes on me. I don't mind. Every comic needs a chance to work on his material. When I was starting out, I used to recite my routines to seagulls and pigeons. And, yes, if birds don't like your jokes, they *will* poop on your shoes.

"Hiya, Jamie," Tony says when he comes to the door with three pepperoni pies. "Good to be here. You know, when Mrs. Smiley called in the pizza

order, she wondered if it would be long. I told her,
'No. It'll be round.'"

Tony looks around behind me nervously. "So is
your cousin Stevie home?"

"Not yet. I think he's still shaking down a few
sixth graders behind the 7-Eleven."

"Good. I'm not saying Stevie's dumb, but one
time, I asked him if he wanted his pizza cut into

six slices or twelve. He said, 'Six. I'm not hungry enough to eat twelve.'"

I laugh. Tony smiles.

"You like my new material?"

"Keep working on it," I say, because I remember some of my early jokes. They came right out of books for first graders, too. The only way to get better at anything is to practice, practice, practice.

Tony takes off. I wheel the pizzas into the dining room, where we wolf down dinner, then settle into our usual spots in the living room for *Jamie Funnie*. Mrs. Smiley cozies up on the couch with Mr. Smiley. Stevie's little brother and sister perch on ottomans. I just sit where I park.

Good news: Stevie still isn't home. I may live to laugh another day.

"You know," says Mrs. Smiley, who's just read the show's plot synopsis in *TV Guide*, "I think it's wonderful that you're playing a teacher in this episode, Jamie. Your grandmother would've been so proud."

She, of course, is talking about my mom's mom, who was also her mom. That's, basically, how you become an aunt.

"Your grandmother was a teacher," Mrs. Smiley says. "Third through fifth grades."

I nod because I remember my grandma, even though she passed away two years before my mom and dad and baby sister did, too.

"Yep, she was definitely a teacher," grumbles Mr. Smiley. "That's why she never had any money."

"Well," says Mrs. Smiley with, believe it or not, the hint of a smile. "That didn't matter to her. Mom always said, 'Instead of making money, I'm trying to make a difference.' And that's what Jamie's doing, too. With his TV show. He's teaching kids all kinds of important lessons."

And then she pops up off the couch and kisses me on the cheek! "We're all so proud of you!" gushes Mrs. Smiley.

I blush. All this praise might've gone to my head.

Except that's when Stevie comes in the front door.

"Where's my pie?" he hollers.

"In the pizza box!" his little brother shouts back.

"I don't want pizza," says Stevie as he stomps into the kitchen. I hear the refrigerator door jiggle open.

Stevie marches into the living room with a frozen Mrs. Jane's apple pie he must've yanked out of the freezer. "I want *this* kind of pie. Just in case anything bad happens to a certain character on *Jamie Not So Funnie* tonight."

Oops.

I think Stevie saw the sneak preview of tonight's episode on YouTube.

He tosses the frozen pie up and down in his hand like he's weighing a cinder block.

I have a funny feeling this one apple pie is going to hurt a lot worse than all the cream pies in Boston.

Chapter 4

SCHOOL DAZE

Fortunately, Aunt Smiley saved me from Stevie's frozen discus to the face.

"You put that pie back in the freezer this instant, young man!" she told him. "I'm saving it for Thanksgiving."

Yes, if I'm still alive, I'm going to be extremely thankful when that holiday rolls around.

And thank ye for not allowing yon bully to slayeth me.

Unfortunately, Aunt Smiley can't protect me from her son (and his buddy Lars) at school.

But that's okay. If Stevie and Lars try to bully me, I'll hit them with a punch line. I figure it's called that because making a bully double over with laughter means he'll have a harder time punching you.

When I roll through the front doors of Long Beach Middle School for the first time in months, I notice that things have definitely changed. Not the smell. It still reeks of antiseptic hand soap mixed with dirty mop water and taco fixings. No, the first thing that strikes me as different is the vice principal—a.k.a. the school's head disciplinarian—standing guard at the door. It's not Mr. Sour Patch, the old guy who used to glare at every kid first thing every morning. It's Ms. Somebody I've Never Met.

"Let's hustle, children," she barks. "Put some pep in your step. Except you, kid in the wheelchair. Pump some rubber! We need to improve our hallway traffic flow rating!"

All of a sudden, Stevie Kosgrov and Lars Johannsen chase a skinny sixth grader down the hall—right in front of the new vice principal.

"Um," I say to the new vice principal, "aren't you going to give those two eighth-grade bullies a detention for picking on that sixth grader?"

"Negative. I have my orders. I'm just a *vice* principal. Gotta do what the big man tells me to do." She gives me a look. "Wait a second. You're Jamie Grimm. The funny boy from TV."

I smile because, hey, it's always cool to be recognized. "Yeah," I say as modestly as I can. "Would you like an autograph?"

"No. I would like for you to quickly and efficiently make your way to your first-period class. You are blocking my avenue of ingress. This is a hallway, not a stall way! Move it, Mr. Grimm. Hustle! I want to see skid marks!"

"Yes, ma'am!" I say. I even salute.

I pump my arms furiously and zoom around the corner, then hit a roadblock.

Two of them, actually.

Stevie and Lars.

Chapter 5

BOOKING IT

My worst nightmares are standing in the hallway with their hands on their hips, glaring at me the way hungry lions glare at gazelles.

The two of them, side by side, are so wide, there's no way I'm getting around them.

"Welcome back to our world, Crip," says Stevie.

"We missed you, Joke Boy," adds Lars.

"Really?" I squeak. "I missed you guys, too. Hey, I have an idea. Let's keep on missing each other. Just pretend I'm not here."

"Oh, you won't be here," says Lars. "Not when we're through with you."

"Yeah," says Stevie. "You'll be in the emergency room."

"No, thanks," I say. "Been there. Done that. Got the T-shirt *and* the hospital gown."

"Is he making a joke?" Lars whispers to Stevie.

"No," snarls Stevie. "He *is* a joke. And I'm about to give him his punch line!"

He balls up his fist.

"Thank you, guys," I say with a smile. "You've been a great crowd. But I've got to go."

I pivot backward, tip up on my rear wheels, spin around, and race down the hall as fast as my arms can push me. Stevie and Lars lumber after me.

"Come back here, Lamie Jamie!" shouts Stevie.

"We're going to break your face!" adds Lars.

I zip past the office, hoping that the principal will see what's going on and stop it.

But the only one behind the counter is the school secretary. She smiles and waves at me with her flower-topped pen.

"Hiya, Jamie. Good to have you back, hon."

I jab a thumb over my shoulder. "Bullies!"

The secretary laughs and keeps waving. "Oh, you're such a joker, Jamie. Have a nice day, hon."

I pump harder.

Stevie and Lars start flinging their textbooks at me. Two whiz past my ears like very thick Frisbees. One lands with a thud on the floor. The other veers left and bangs into a locker.

But the books give me an idea.

I need to seek sanctuary in the one place the two bullies would never think to look: the library. Lars and Stevie never use books for anything but weapons, so I'm guessing they don't even know the school *has* a library!

I round a corner, shove open a pair of glass doors, and slam on the brakes in the reference section, where I can hide behind a bookcase filled with encyclopedias.

I hear Stevie and Lars skid to a sneaker-squeaking halt in the hallway.

"Where'd he go?" says Stevie.

"I dunno," says Lars. "What's this room here?"

"I'm not sure. But it smells like books."

"Gross."

"Totally."

"Let's get out of here. I'm allergic to books."

"Me too."

The two giants clump down the hall.

I'm safe.

For now, anyway.

To be honest, I don't really use the library all that much. Except for hiding. It really is a bully-free zone because no self-respecting bully would ever voluntarily enter a room with so many books on the shelves.

I decide to stay a little longer and search the stacks. I'm hoping I can find a good book. Something like *Wheelchair Karate for Dummies*.

Chapter 6

SHOWTIME BY THE SEA

I manage to avoid Stevie and Lars for the rest of the day.

After school, I want to keep on avoiding Stevie, so I head down the boardwalk to Uncle Frankie's Good Eats by the Sea. As I'm rolling along, swerving through the flocks of squawking seagulls, I'm soaking up more than the sunshine. When you're a comic, you're always on the lookout for new material. Especially if you're starring in a sitcom that needs ideas for eleven more episodes!

For instance, there's this one guy I pass almost every day—Crazy Bob. That's what he calls himself. It's even printed on the sheet of cardboard he uses for a sign. Crazy Bob likes to stand on the boardwalk and warn everybody about the coming alien invasion.

I always toss a quarter into Crazy Bob's tin cup. Hey, if the Galaxatronians show up next week, I want to be in good with their earthly ambassador.

I roll into the diner, and Uncle Frankie greets me with a flick of his yo-yo and a big smile.

"Hiya, kiddo. How was school?"

"Weird," I say. "So much has changed since we've been in the studio doing the TV show."

"Really?" says Uncle Frankie with a sly grin. "Are you sure *you're* not the one who's changed?"

"Positive. I've been wearing this same puffy vest since forever. In fact, the 1980s called. Said they wanted it back."

Frankie laughs.

"You ready to take the stage?" he asks.

"You bet."

I roll to my usual spot behind the cash register just as Mrs. Sowicky, one of our regulars, shuffles up to the counter.

"Hi, Mrs. S. Can I get you anything else?"

She knows I'm not talking about dessert or a cup of coffee to go. You see, after the horrible car crash that put me in my chair, I spent a lot of time at a hospital called the Hope Trust Rehabilitation Center. The doctors there really believed in laughter being the best medicine. So, after the surgeries and in between physical therapy sessions, I spent my days reading joke books, watching comedy videos, and memorizing the routines of the world's greatest comedians. At the diner, I've become our joke jukebox. A customer picks a comedian; I play some of their greatest hits.

"How about a little George Carlin?" says Mrs. Sowicky.

"No problem. 'Beethoven was so hard of hearing he thought he was a painter.'" I hit the cash register keys to give myself a *bada-bing* rim shot.

Mrs. Sowicky smiles, so I give her a second helping of Carlin. "When cheese has its picture taken, what does it say? Isn't it a bit unnerving that doctors call what they do 'practice'?"

I hand Mrs. S. her change. She plunks the coins into the tip jar.

"Thanks, Jamie. Good to have you back. Love your show!"

I love it, too. But the show I do when I'm just horsing around at Uncle Frankie's? I love it even more!

As the tip jar fills up, the diner door swings open and in walks a lady with curly red hair.

Out of the corner of my eye, I can see Uncle Frankie slipping on his special gold-colored yo-yo— the flashy one with the blinking LEDs inside. They swirl when he twirls.

Hmm. Uncle Frankie pulls out Goldie only for special occasions.

I'm thinking the lady with the curly red hair who just floated through the door is just that: someone special!

Chapter 7

HEART ON A STRING

In case you forgot, Uncle Frankie used to be the junior yo-yo champion of Brooklyn. He won a trophy shaped like a giant yo-yo, complete with a golden string. It made it easy to tug around the house.

Uncle Frankie still knows all the flicks and flourishes. He can do Walk the Dog, Rock the Baby, Barrel Roll, Lindy Loop, Split the Atom, Pop 'n' Fresh, and Gravity Pull without blinking an eye.

For the lady with the curly red hair, he does them all. Simultaneously.

Uncle Frankie finishes with a grand, backward, upside-down, through-his-legs spin of the yo-yo,

without breaking any glasses or sending the silverware flying!

"Fantastic, Francis!" says the lady.

"Thank you, Flora," says Uncle Frankie, taking a slight bow.

I applaud. Flora looks over at me.

"You're Jamie!" she says with a big smile.

"Yeah," I say, blushing a little. (I'm still not used to strangers recognizing me.) "I guess you've seen my TV show, huh?"

"No, sorry. I don't watch much TV. Too many books to read! But I have heard all about you." She turns to Uncle Frankie. "Francis told me everything! How you won that comedy contest, how you helped him out after the hurricane, how you help out all sorts of charities. How you're the best nephew in the whole wide world."

Okay. Now I'm blushing so much, my ears feel like a pair of red-hot toaster coils.

"Flora—I mean, uh, Ms. Denning just moved to Long Beach," says Frankie. "She's the new librarian at your school."

"Seriously?" I say. "I was just in the library this morning."

"Really?" says Ms. Denning. "I didn't see you."

"Good!"

"Excuse me?"

"I was sort of hiding."

She smiles. "Then you were doing a very good job of it."

Uncle Frankie raises a single eyebrow and crinkles his forehead. "Why were you hiding in the library, Jamie?"

"All the toilet stalls were already full," I joke, because I don't want to tell Uncle Frankie the truth about Stevie gunning for me again. After all, he's Stevie's uncle, too, and I don't feel like getting the whole family involved.

"Well, Jamie," says Ms. Denning, "you're welcome to hide out in the library anytime you like. And bring your friends. Please."

She does it like Henny Youngman delivering his classic joke: "Take my wife. *Please.*"

"That would be good if you could, Jamie," says Uncle Frankie. "Maybe you, Gilda, Gaynor, and Pierce can hit the library on a regular basis now that you guys are back in school for a few weeks.

You should encourage the other kids to use the library more often, too. Flora's got all sorts of books in there."

My turn to arch an eyebrow. It's a library. Of course it has books.

But I can tell Uncle Frankie isn't using his brain right now. His heart is currently in charge. He is seriously crushing on Ms. Flora Denning.

"I'd appreciate it if you and your friends could drop by," says Ms. Denning.

"Me too," says Uncle Frankie, gesturing with his finger for me to roll closer so he can tell me a secret. "They might shut down the library."

I guess I'm not the only one who hasn't been using the library all that much lately. What can I say? I have an iPhone. I Google.

"Coach Ball isn't a big fan," says Ms. Denning.

"That's too bad," I say. "Um, who's Coach Ball?"

"Your new principal," says Uncle Frankie.

"Our principal's first name is Coach?"

"He used to teach phys ed," explains Ms. Denning. "He likes being called Coach instead of Principal. He wants to convince the school board that our library space could be better used for other purposes."

"Like what?" I ask.

She shrugs. "Something without books, I guess."

Chapter 8

BASKETBALL COURT JESTER

I was bummed to hear that some people want to shut down the school library, but to be honest, it isn't a major concern of mine.

Like I said, I've never used the school library all that much. Just the joke book section. So I don't have to worry about Ms. Denning's dilemma.

Which is good because I have a ton of other stuff to worry about.

Did I mention that we have to come up with ideas for eleven more *Jamie Funnie* episodes? Yes, the show has writers, but they're always asking me for ideas. I've been thinking it might be fun to do a show about me signing up for murderball—that's a little like wheelchair basketball and it's insanely intense.

So, on Tuesday night, I go to a basketball game with Gilda, Gaynor, and Pierce—Long Beach Middle versus our rivals from Valley Stream—to do a little research. We, of course, get courtside seats. Not because we're TV stars or celebrities. No, we're courtside because it's really, really, *really* hard (okay, impossible) for me to climb bleachers in my wheelchair. Climbing Mount Everest would be easier. At least mountains don't have steps. Their ramps are made out of rock.

"So, guess what I learned from Uncle Frankie?" I say to my buds.

"What?" says Gilda. "A new recipe for deep-fried bacon?"

"No. The new principal and the school board are thinking about closing the library."

"Cool," says Gaynor. "Are they going to, like, repaint it or something?"

"No. They want to shut it down forever and use the room for something else."

"That's ridiculous," says Gilda. "We need the library. How do you think I learned so much about making movies? It wasn't in math class. It was in the library."

"I enjoy the wide assortment of manga and graphic novels," adds Pierce. "You can't learn very much about alien civilizations and supervillains in history textbooks."

"Well," I say, "I'm sure it's just a rumor. Even if not many kids use it, no way can you have a middle school without a library."

"Unless you give every kid a free iPad," says Gaynor. "Free iPads would be awesome."

Vincent O'Neil, a kid who still cracks the corniest jokes this side of Nebraska (the Cornhusker State), sees us sitting courtside and comes over to entertain us with his latest string of one-liners. When I first met Vincent, he used to tell everybody he was ten billion times funnier than me. Now he just tells everybody the jokes he memorizes out of joke books.

"Looking forward to the B-ball game?" Vincent asks, and I just know he's memorized a whole slew of basketball jokes off some website.

"Yep," says Gaynor.

And that's all Vincent needs to launch into his routine.

"You know, Gilda," says Vincent. "You remind me of Cinderella."

"Whaaat?"

Vincent ignores her death glare and bulldozes ahead to his punch line. "Cinderella wanted to play basketball, but the coach kicked her off the team because she kept running away from the ball. Get it? In the fairy tale, Cinderella runs—"

"We got it," says Gilda.

"Hey, you know what they call a Long Beach Middle School basketball player with a trophy?" Vincent goes on.

I take the bait. "What?"

"A senior citizen. This school hasn't won a championship in thirty years! And then, it was for showing up and playing nice."

That one actually makes me grin. "Hey, Vincent," I say.

"Yeah?"

"Gilda and I might brainstorm ideas for new *Jamie Funnie* episodes tomorrow after school. Want to join us?"

"Me? Help you guys? Writing jokes for *Jamie Funnie*?"

"Sure. It'll be fun."

Gilda gives me a look. And a knee nudge. And maybe a toe stomp. (I can't feel those.)

Yes, she thinks I'm insane. But, well, I sort of feel sorry for Vincent.

"Just tell me when and where," he says, sounding super psyched.

"How about the library?" says Gilda. "Nobody ever goes there, so we can have the place to ourselves."

"Awesome! You guys are the best."

Vincent knocks knuckles with me and Gilda,

then climbs the bleachers to tell his basketball jokes to somebody else.

"Thanks," I tell Gilda.

"You owe me one," she says with a sideways grin. "Actually, you might owe me *two*. Maybe, if we're lucky, the new librarian will come over and shush Vincent when he starts telling jokes."

"Nah," I said. "I met her at the diner. She's too nice to shush."

"What?" says Gaynor. "How can you be a librarian if you don't tell kids to keep quiet? Shushing is totally in the job description! They learn finger-lip coordination at library school!"

Chapter 9

MORE BASKETBALL JOKES

Speaking of jokes...

I hate to say it, but the Long Beach Middle School basketball team is pretty horrible. And from what everybody tells me, they've been horrible for years.

You know those teams that go on tour to play against the Harlem Globetrotters? Their losing streak is something like 2,495 games. The Long Beach Middle School Minnows have a losing streak that's closer to 3,000.

It'd be funny if it weren't so sad.

We're down by twenty-nine points at halftime. The cheerleaders aren't leading cheers. They're too busy weeping into their pom-poms.

I hear a speaker squeal with feedback and then a *THUMP-THUMP-THUMP*.

A big barrel of a man with a flattop hairdo, wearing a tracksuit and squeaky black sneakers, marches out to center court with a long microphone cable trailing behind him. He taps the microphone again to make sure it's working. *THUMP-THUMP-THUMP*.

"Students?" he booms to the bleachers. "Sit down. Parents, too!"

Everybody immediately does what he says. The

guy has that kind of voice. Plus, he's squinting and scowling and heavy mouth-breathing into the microphone. He reminds me of Darth Vader—but with a double chin and no neck.

"That's the guy who wants to shut down the library," whispers Gilda. "Coach Ball. Our new principal."

"People," says Coach Ball, pacing back and forth like a general. "I am your new commander in chief here at Long Beach Middle School. As such, I plan on ushering in a new era of sporting excellence. We will no longer be the laughingstock of Long Island interscholastic athletics. We will be champions!"

There is a smattering of terrified applause.

Coach Ball breathes into the microphone again. "Speaking of unwanted laughter…"

Uh-oh.

He's looking right at me.

"I am not amused by the antics of a certain clique of smart-mouth, smart-aleck, smarty-pants kids making fun of *my* middle school on national television."

He does that thing where he points two fingers at his eyes, flicks them around to point at me, and flips them back to point at his eyes again.

"You are on my radar, Mr. Grimm. Word of advice? You do *not* want to be on my radar. Bad things happen if you are. *BEEP-BEEP, BOOM!*"

I think he's imitating a radar. And some kind of guided missile.

He puts his whistle to his lips and blows a shrill blast. "Johannsen? Kosgrov? Front and center. Now!"

Can this get any worse? Stevie Kosgrov and Lars Johannsen join Coach Ball at center court. They are both wearing chin-strapped headgear that looks like earmuffs made out of football pads.

"Ladies and gentlemen," says our new principal, "we may not have the talent to field a football team or to win at basketball. But we've definitely got the talent to put Long Beach Middle School in the state wrestling finals this year! Especially in the heavyweight division."

He claps Stevie and Lars on the back.

"If you're tough enough and fast enough to join these two fine gentlemen, come try out for the team. I'll be the coach, and let me make this perfectly clear: I'll do whatever it takes to win!"

What happens when the basketball game starts up again?

We lose.

Chapter 10

DOUBLE GROANERS

The next day at school, I have a free period, so I swing by the library to check in with Ms. Denning.

Now that I have a little time to look around, I notice she's already made a few changes. Everything seems brighter. More fun. She has a display of books that are MS. D.'S FAVES AND RAVES set up on a table in the middle of the room. There's also a sign-up sheet for a brand-new Battle of the Books team. She even has a trivia question written on a whiteboard: *Who are the four Kidd kids in the book* Treasure Hunters?

"And over there," she says when she sees me checking out the new additions, "is where I plan to put the 3-D printer and our makerspace."

"Cool. When's that going to happen?"

"Right after I win the lottery."

"That would be so awesome."

"It would, wouldn't it?" she says with a smile. "I also wish we had a few windows."

Whoever designed this school gave the library glass doors but windowless cinder-block walls. The only lighting is the greenish glow from fluorescent fixtures in the ceiling.

"So, Jamie, did you come in here to hide today?"

"No. I just wanted to officially say 'hi' and 'welcome to Long Beach Middle School.' I was new here last year. I know how tough that can be."

"Thanks. Any tips?"

"Yes. Stay away from the French-bread pizza in the cafeteria. Unless you like burning the roof of your mouth while simultaneously chewing soggy slippers."

She laughs. "I'll try to remember that."

"Hey, Jamie!"

Vincent O'Neil pops out from behind a wall of shelves. He's thumbing through the pages of a very thick book. Yep. It's a joke book.

"Hey, Jamie—guess what kind of books planets like to read?" he asks me.

I grimace and give him the corny answer: "Comet books."

"Oh. Okay. You've heard that one." He thumbs through the book. "Here's another...."

"See you later, Jamie!" says Vincent. "I need to study some more joke books before our brainstorming session after school!"

He disappears behind the bookcases. I whisper to Ms. Denning: "Another tip? You might want to limit Vincent to one joke book per day!"

She winks and shoots me a silent *Okay*.

The bell rings and I roll off to my next class.

When I hit the hallway, I see Stevie Kosgrov standing on top of a water fountain like he's ready

to pounce on the next person who passes by. He's wearing a ski mask. Lars Johannsen is on the other side of the hall, slamming a metal chair against a steel locker. He's wearing a ski mask, too. A crowd of terrified kids are frozen around them, like they're in the ring at a WWE wrestling match.

Why do I think I'm about to be body-slammed?

Chapter 11

LET'S GET READY TO RUUUUUMBLE

I need a victim!" shouts Stevie, teetering on his water fountain perch.

So Lars grabs one of the spectators, a quivering sixth grader, and hurls him into the ring of kids. Stevie leaps off the water fountain and drops the poor boy to the floor.

"Hey, Stevie!" I shout as I roll into the center of the ring. "Pick on someone your own size—like that Bob's Big Boy statue."

"Grimm!" Stevie snarls through his mask mouth hole.

"Time for a Choke-Slam Brainbuster!" shouts Lars.

Stevie assumes some kind of sumo wrestler pose. "With a Dunking Dogleg Dump-Truck Twist!"

He and Lars are both on me in a flash.

"Double-teaming!" shouts a kid in the crowd. "That's against the rules. One of you has to tag out!"

Stevie and Lars ignore the WWE fan *and* the wrestling rule book. Together, they rock my chair forward and toss me out of my seat like you'd toss out the trash. I end up sprawled on the floor, flat on my face.

They're going to turn me into Flat Jamie. I close my eyes and brace for impact.

But then I hear the screech of a gym whistle. I creak open one eye and can see squeaky black sneakers creeping down the hall.

It's the new principal!

I'm saved!

"Gentlemen," barks Coach Ball, "what you are doing is completely wrong!"

Phew.

I knew, no matter how nutty the principal is about "interscholastic athletics" (which sounds like some sort of game at the book fair), no way would he let bullies terrorize innocent kids in the hallways.

Coach Ball marches right up to Stevie and Lars and leans in. "One hundred percent, completely, totally wrong."

I'm still on my belly, flat on the floor. My chair is ten feet behind me, lying on its side with the top wheel spinning.

"I was hoping you'd say something, Coach Ball," says Mr. Getzler, one of the best teachers at Long Beach Middle School, as he comes out of his physics lab. Mr. Getzler teaches students how to build Ping-

Pong ball catapults so we can learn about force, momentum, and nailing the garbage can for three points.

Coach Ball glares at Mr. Getzler.

"Little help?" I peep.

Everybody completely ignores me because they're too busy quaking in their shoes, boots, and penny loafers. Coach Ball is giving them all a dark, icy stare. He's good. The guy must've studied glowering at college.

"Where was I before Mr. Getzler so rudely interrupted me?" he asks.

"Uh, you were telling us how wrong we were for beating up little kids," grunts Lars.

"And how bad it is to throw my cousin out of his wheelchair?" adds Stevie.

Coach Ball shakes his bristle-brush head. "That's not what I'm angry about, boys. On the contrary, I applaud your initiative. You're eager to get started. But this is the wrong kind of wrestling! We're not talking about that made-up monkey business on TV. We're talking Olympic-style Greco-Roman wrestling!"

He grabs hold of poor Mr. Getzler, who probably wishes he never stepped out of his classroom.

"Here's how you execute a two-point takedown."

He puts his leg behind Mr. Getzler's leg, twists him sideways, and hauls him down to the floor.

"Then you need to flip him over, pin his shoulders to the mat, and hold him there for a count of three!"

"One, two, three!" chant Stevie and Lars when Mr. Getzler stops squirming and lets Coach Ball press his shoulders to the floor.

"That's a pin and that's how you win," says Coach Ball.

He stands up and dusts off his sweatpants.

"You okay, Getzler?"

"Well, my head sort of hurts...."

"Don't be such a crybaby. If you're hurt, go see the school nurse. Maybe she'll give you a lollipop."

"Yes, sir."

Coach Ball drapes his arms around Stevie's and Lars's shoulders.

"What we need is a proper training facility to teach you boys the fundamentals of Olympic-style wrestling."

"You mean like the gym?" says Lars.

"We could take it away from the basketball team," suggests Stevie. "They stink so bad, they don't need to practice."

Coach Ball shakes his head. "The gym is where we'll host our matches. But for training, we need a wrestling room. Someplace without windows but plenty of space to lay down mats."

"The faculty lounge doesn't have any windows," moans Mr. Getzler.

I guess when you're a teacher, you have to stay on the principal's good side no matter what.

"Excellent suggestion, Getzler," says the new principal. "Come on, team. Let's hit the faculty lounge." He pounds his fist into his hand. "It's time to clear out a few coffeepots!"

Chapter 12

CLOUDY WITH A CHANCE OF SPITBALLS

After school, Gilda, Vincent O'Neil, and I meet up in the library to spitball ideas for new *Jamie Funnie* episodes.

"Should I go to the cafeteria and grab a straw?" asks Vincent. "For the spitballing?"

"It's just a term," I say. "We all toss out ideas. Then we see which ones stick to the walls."

"Cool."

"And Vincent?" says Gilda.

"Yeah?"

"We don't need jokes right now. Just story ideas."

"Oh. Okay. So I guess you don't want to know

what washes up on very small, teeny-tiny beaches."

I think about it for half a second. "Microwaves?"

"Yeah," says Vincent sadly.

Gilda tries her best not to groan. Really, she does. It's hard.

"You guys need anything?" asks Ms. Denning as she walks past our table rolling a cart filled with books she's going to reshelve.

"No," I say. "But thanks for keeping the library open after school."

"No problem. In fact, I'm thinking about staying open for a couple of extra hours every day. Hosting some new activities."

"That'd be great," I say. "Not everybody has a diner to hang out in like I do."

"Will you be there tonight?" she asks.

"Yep. The blue plate special is meat loaf."

"That's the problem with meat," cracks Vincent. "It's so lazy. Always loafing around."

"Well, have fun, guys," says Ms. Denning. "See you at the diner, Jamie!" She trundles away with her cart.

"She's nice," says Gilda.

I nod. "Uncle Frankie would definitely agree."

"Yeah," says Vincent. "I'll be super sad when they fire her."

"Whaaat?" says Gilda.

"Haven't you guys heard? The new principal wants to shut down the library. If you don't have a library, you don't really need a librarian. Hey, speaking of librarians…"

Hoo-boy. Here we go again.

"Do you guys know how many librarians it takes to screw in a lightbulb?"

"No," says Gilda with a sigh.

"Neither do the librarians," says Vincent. "But they all know how to look up the answer!"

That's when Principal (I mean *Coach*) Ball marches into the library with a whole slew of people wearing suits.

"This is the spare room I was telling you about," says Coach Ball. "The Internet and Google have made libraries obsolete. We don't need a room full of dusty books and encyclopedias."

"Actually," says Ms. Bumgarten, "a library is very—"

"Bumgarten," snarls Coach Ball.

"Sir?"

"When I want your opinion, I'll give it to you."

"Yes, sir."

"As I was saying, we don't really need a library anymore. We just need a couple of computers—which we already have in the tech lab."

"A school without a library?" says a lady in a business suit. "I don't know...."

"The kids won't miss it, Mrs. Critchett," says

Coach Ball. "Heck, there's never anybody in here anyhow."

"We're in here!" says Gilda, standing up defiantly.

"I meant normal students," sneers Coach Ball. "Not two smart alecks and a wisenheimer."

"Which one of us is the wisenheimer?" asks Vincent.

"Whoever I say it is!"

"Right. Gotcha. Thanks."

Coach Ball makes his pitch to the suits. "Look, Mrs. Critchett, being president of the school board means you need to think about Long Beach Middle's future, not its past. Well, the future has already left this library behind. That's why we should repurpose this space that nobody wants or needs and turn it into a practice facility. A sweat room for my new wrestling team!"

Ms. Denning comes out from behind a bookcase.

"Do you know which American president often talked about his wrestling days as a young man in Illinois?"

"No, Ms. Denning," fumes Coach Ball. "And frankly, I don't care. Neither does anybody else."

"Abraham Lincoln," says Ms. Denning pleasantly.

"I learned that right here, today, in this library."

"Really? Well, I could've learned it in two seconds with Google!"

"I just did," says one of the school board guys, fiddling with his phone. "And did you know that the longest Olympic wrestling contest ever was the 1912 semifinal bout between Martin Klein for Russia and Alfred Asikainen of Finland, which went on for almost twelve hours?"

"No," admits Ms. Denning.

Me? I'm trying to imagine the stink in the air after that eleven-hour wrestling match.

Chapter 13

JOKES TO THE RESCUE!

The library is the heart and soul of any school," insists Ms. Denning.

"Agreed," says Ms. Bumgarten. "And if I may add—"

"No, you may not," says Coach Ball, cutting her off again. I guess speaking isn't a job requirement for vice principals.

Ms. Denning courageously keeps going. "The school library is the one place where kids can expand their horizons and independently study whatever interests they wish to pursue."

"Well, who wants them doing that?" says Coach Ball. "Students should be at their desks studying what the school board tells them to study so they can get ready for their state standardized tests! They shouldn't be in here daydreaming and thinking on their own!"

"Jamie?" pleads Gilda.

Uh-oh. When I glance over at her, she has that *Do something!* look in her eye.

And I think she wants me to do it *now*.

Of course, she's probably right. Shutting down the school library might be wrong, foolish, and imprudent—a word I just learned by cracking open the library's ginormous thesaurus. If Coach Ball gets rid of the school's library, it could be a huge mistake. I couldn't stand the thought of all these books getting thrown out to make room for wrestling mats. (Actually, I *can't* stand for anything, but you get the idea.)

It's time to roll into action.

I back away from the table and whirl around to face my audience.

"Hiya, folks. I'm Jamie Grimm."

Yep. It's time for a command performance, even if there are only eight people in the crowd.

I go for my big finish.

"Speaking for all the students at Long Beach Middle School—which is extremely hard to do unless you're the best ventriloquist in the world— we *need* this library, ladies and gentlemen! We cannot let it close! Let the wrestling team sweat somewhere else. I suggest Miami. In August. They can all visit their grandmothers at the same time. Thank you! I'm Jamie Grimm, and you've been a great crowd!"

Coach Ball is scowling at me.

Again.

The school board members (and Ms. Denning) are smiling and clapping. They loved my impromptu stand-up bit!

"You're Jamie Grimm!" gushes one lady. "I'm Lexi Critchett! I know you!"

"From TV!" gushes another member of the board.

"You funny!" they all gush together.

"Maybe we should give this matter further consideration before turning the library into a sweat room, Coach Ball," says Mrs. Critchett, who, I'm pretty sure, is in charge of the school board. Which means she's Coach Ball's boss.

Yes!

I think we might've just bought Ms. Denning and the library a little extra time. I know for certain that I've just made a very powerful enemy.

One with a flattop haircut and a closet full of tracksuits.

Coach Ball is eyeballing me like I'm a gnat and he's the windshield.

Maybe I should just go ahead and change my Google name to SplatOnWheels567.

Chapter 19

DINOSAUR ROAR

You people are just trying to avoid the inevitable!" Coach Ball snarls at the school board members. "This library is a dinosaur."

"I respectfully disagree," I say, trying to blink some of the flop sweat out of my eyes. What can I say? Authority figures make me nervous. I don't do well with confrontation, either.

But I keep going.

Mostly because Gilda looks so worried. The library is her sanctuary.

"If this library were a dinosaur," I say, "it'd be a lot louder and have stubby little arms." I start doing my best *T. rex* impression.

"If this library is a dinosaur, we should definitely keep it. Because in a couple of million years, it'll be a big pool of oil and we'll all be filthy rich!"

When I'm done riffing on dinosaurs, I move on to the important stuff.

"This is the one place in the whole building where we students can come to think for ourselves. The one place where I, Jamie Grimm, can choose exactly what I want to study. For instance, the history of the knock-knock joke."

Coach Ball is sputtering mad. "What?"

"Did you know," I say, "that before there were knock-knock jokes, there were do-you-know jokes?"

"No," says Gilda, trying to help me out. "I did not know about do-you-know jokes."

"Here's one from around 1900," I say. "Do you know Arthur?"

"Arthur who?" says Gilda.

"Arthurmometer!"

The board members chuckle.

"After the do-you-know era came the have-you-ever-heard-of jokes in the 1920s. For instance, have you ever heard of Hiawatha?"

"Hiawatha who?" asks Gilda.

"Hiawatha a lonely boy until I met you!"

More laughter. From everybody except Coach Ball, of course.

"In the 1930s, 'Have you ever heard of' became 'Knock, knock. Who's there?,' and the rest, as they say, is history."

"Who cares?" snarls Coach Ball.

"Me!" I tell him. "That's my point: I might be the only kid in the whole entire school who gives two hoots about this particular historical tidbit, but here in the library, I can do my own independent research on any subject I want. Lots of kids come in here all the time to read books on their own interests." Okay, that might be a bit of a stretch, unless my friends count as a lot. "That's why the library needs to stay a library."

"You make a good argument," says one of the board members. "My kids love your show. So do I. It's must-see TV every Friday night at our house."

"Thank you, Mrs. Critchett."

"Coach Ball," she says, turning to him. "Let's make a deal."

"What sort of a deal?"

"A compromise."

"I don't like those. Compromising means I have to give something up."

"Please. Hear me out," Mrs. Critchett says to Coach Ball. "If your new librarian, Ms. Denning, can prove by the end of the month that a majority of your students are using the library, then the library will stay a library and your new wrestling room will go downstairs in the basement, in that empty area behind the boiler room."

"That's a crawl space!"

"You said you didn't want any windows," says another board member.

Knock, knock!

Um, who's there?

Nobody. That's just me knocking your head against the dirt floor!

"The floor down there is nothing but dirt and rocks!"

"You can put down wrestling mats," I suggest.

Bad idea.

Coach Ball glares at me, harder than he's ever glared at anyone before.

The new principal and me?

We are never, *ever* going to be besties.

Chapter 15

WHAT HAVE YOU DONE WITH UNCLE FRANKIE?

After school, I head to the diner to tell Uncle Frankie the news: Ms. Denning has till the end of the month to prove how popular the school library can be. Less than four weeks to turn it from an empty wasteland into something with crowds the size of Disneyland!

"Indeed," says Uncle Frankie, not sounding like Uncle Frankie at all. "Flora hath texted me with said news. It's a bit of a sticky wicket, eh, what?"

He doesn't look like Uncle Frankie, either. Instead of his usual short-order cook outfit, he is wearing a tweed jacket with patches on the elbows,

a vest, and a bow tie. He's also wearing horn-rimmed smart-guy glasses.

"Since when do you wear glasses?" I ask him.

"It is a recent sartorial addition."

"Huh?"

He looks around to make sure nobody is listening. "I started wearing 'em yesterday. Picked 'em up at the drug store. The lenses are just plain glass, but they make me look smarter."

No. They make him look nearsighted.

I sniff the air.

It smells like sputtering burger grease mixed with Old Spice cologne. I think Uncle Frankie dunked his head in a bucket of the stuff. The cologne, not the burger drippings.

"So, um, what's going on?" I ask.

Uncle Frankie motions for me to join him in the back room.

"I'm trying to class myself up a little, Jamie," he tells me when we're back with the mops and pickle tubs. "The diner, too. I want to turn Good Eats by the Sea into the kind of restaurant a refined literary lady such as your new librarian, Ms. Denning, would feel comfortable in. I'm thinking about putting tablecloths on all the tables. Maybe candles. I might even change the doo-wop music in the jukebox to some of that classical stuff. You know—Mozart, Beethoven, Elvis."

"Seriously?"

"I'm changing up the menu, too. Instead of flapjacks and OJ, we could serve Mark Twain Whole Grain Pancakes and Dr. Seuss Juice. I think Flora would like that. Are there any books with hamburger in the title?"

"I'll have to check the card catalog," I say.

"Thank you, Jamie," he sighs.

If this were a cartoon, little hearts and tweeting bluebirds would be swirling around his head right now.

No doubt about it: Uncle Frankie is seriously smitten with our new librarian.

He's been a widower for a long time and hasn't had a girlfriend in years. Might be why he's kind of rusty on the whole romance thing.

"One more thing," says Uncle Frankie. "Maybe instead of telling jokes behind the register, you could quote Shakespeare or something. Maybe some of them poets like Robert Defrost."

"You mean Robert *Frost?*"

"Either one." He checks his phone. "Ms. Denning is on her way. She needs someone to hold her hand in this time of crisis."

"She also needs a ton more kids to start using her library."

"So I heard. You've got to help her out in that department, kiddo." Uncle Frankie is giving me puppy-dog eyes. "Ms. Denning just got to town. I don't want her leaving before she falls...before..."

"Before what?"

"Before, uh, the big Polar Bear Plunge on Super Bowl Sunday."

Yep. Uncle Frankie is a rusty romantic and a very bad liar.

Chapter 16

TAKE A WALK ON THE BOARDWALK (I WISH I COULD)

Uncle Frankie has never asked me for anything before.

Usually he's the one giving *me* stuff—like his classic cherry-red 1967 Mustang convertible and great life advice. Plus, Uncle Frankie's the one who first told me about the Planet's Funniest Kid Comic Contest, because he said I had a comedic gift. If it weren't for him, I wouldn't be where I am today.

Which is on the boardwalk. After dark.

It's pretty clear that Uncle Frankie is counting

on me to help keep Ms. Denning, the new love of his life, in town. That's a pretty heavy responsibility. And the boardwalk is where I go whenever I need to ponder serious, weighty issues: Why am I here? Why don't woodpeckers get headaches? Why are there no B batteries?

Somehow, Cool Girl—my strangely wise and Yoda-esque friend from school—always knows when I'm stuck in one of these emotional jams. It's like she can read my mind and mysteriously shows up on the boardwalk just to lend me an ear. We'll sit on our special bench under a streetlamp while I talk out whatever's bugging me.

Well, *she* sits on it. I sit next to it.

Cool Girl is what I call her because she's so cool. She's also a girl. (Yes, we have kissed. Twice.) Her real name is Suzie Orolvsky. Cool Girl is a lot easier to pronounce.

I roll closer to the bench and I can see her silhouette.

Yep, as always, she's there.

Waiting for me.

Except…

Cool Girl doesn't wear a baseball cap.

And her hair is straight, not a frizzy mop.

"Hiya, Jamie."

It's Gilda Gold.

"Um, what are you doing out here?" I ask her.

She shrugs. "I don't know. This is where I always come when I have, you know, stuff to think about."

"What's on your mind?" I ask, wheeling closer.

"School. How much it's changed since we've been away."

"Yeah. That's been bothering me, too. Especially that crazy new principal."

"And the nonsense about closing down the library," says Gilda, "is the absolute worst."

"I know. Uncle Frankie is really, really, *really* upset about it."

"Huh? He doesn't even go to Long Beach Middle. Why's he so worried about it?"

"Oh. Uh, I think he has, like, a mad crush on Ms. Denning, the new librarian. If they close her library, she'll lose her job. If she loses her job, she'll probably have to move to a new town, one where the middle school still has a library. If that happens, it'll break Uncle Frankie's heart, and he already had a heart attack, so I don't know how much more breakage his heart can take."

"So, does Ms. Denning know how your uncle feels about her?"

"I think so. I mean, he's pretty obvious about it. He wore glasses and a tweed jacket to work tonight."

"That's a sign you're in love?"

My turn to shrug. "I guess. In the adult world, anyway."

"Okay," says Gilda. "Your choice is clear. You're a celebrity. Celebrities have certain powers. You need to do everything and anything you can to help save the library, to get more than fifty percent of the student body using it. You have only twenty-three days. This is more important than brainstorming ideas for your show. The whole school is counting on you. So's your uncle."

"Yeah. Thanks. I guess I knew all that. I just needed to hear somebody else say it."

Gilda smiles. "He was wearing a tweed sport coat behind the grill?"

"Yep."

"Isn't love funny?"

Uh-oh. Gilda is giving me this dreamy kind of look.

I wonder if I'm supposed to kiss *her.*

Chapter 17

CIRCUS SNACKS TO THE RESCUE!

No, I did not kiss Gilda Gold while you were busy flipping pages.

But the very next day, I have a brainstorm about how to draw more kids into the library.

"Free popcorn and cotton candy!" I tell Gilda, Gaynor, and Pierce. "Remember when we did that *Jamie Funnie* episode about going to the Big Apple Circus in New York?"

"'Belly Flop Under the Big Top,'" says Gilda. "Episode six."

"Exactly!"

"Your wheelchair tipped forward and you fell face-first into that pile of elephant poop!" laughs Gaynor. "It was awesome."

"Actually," I say, "it was a bucket of mashed potatoes and brown food coloring."

"I wondered why it smelled so delicious," remarks Pierce.

"We had that popcorn popper and cotton candy machine for that one scene near the ticket booth," I continue. "I bet if we call the prop guys, they'll haul 'em both out here to Long Beach."

"Worth a shot," says Gilda.

She whips out her phone. Since she's directed over half of the episodes so far, she is tight with all the crew people. She chats with the props mistress, Nancy Graziano.

Three hours later, the popcorn and cotton candy machines are up and running in the library. The smell of hot, freshly popped popcorn wafting down the halls of the school? Stronger than any scent in the world. Except maybe cinnamon buns at the mall.

I go into total carnival barker mode.

"Get your books and buttery popcorn, folks. Step right up. Free popcorn and cotton candy with every book. Check it out and then check 'em out."

Kids are streaming into the library like crazy. Pierce is stationed near the door with one of those little hand clickers for counting people.

"We're up to one hundred and twenty-three students, seven teachers, two lunch ladies, and Gus, the janitor."

"Um, Jamie," says Ms. Denning, "I'm not sure this is such a great idea."

"Are you kidding?" I say. "Look at this crowd! If we can keep doing these kinds of publicity stunts every day for a month, they're not going to close down the library, they're going to need to expand it!"

That's when Stevie and Lars all of a sudden

discover that their school has a library.

"How come it smells like a movie theater in here?" demands Stevie.

"A movie theater at the county fair," adds Lars.

Then the two of them see the popcorn popper, which is in the middle of cooking up a fresh batch. Kernels are exploding inside the kettle like a string of firecrackers.

Lars and Stevie push and shove their way to the center of the room.

"Set it free!" shouts Stevie, swinging open the little glass door and lifting the lid on the corn-popping kettle.

A barrage of hot popcorn and sizzling seeds shoots out of the machine.

Meanwhile, Lars is over at the cotton candy machine. He lifts off its plastic dome and chucks it to the floor.

He also hits the ULTRAHIGH WHIP button.

The swirling sugar cyclone in the center of the cart flings stringy shreds of sticky pink sugar over the edges of the stainless steel tub. Strands of gummy, gluey gunk—looking like out-of-control attic insulation—spatter kids, books, and furniture.

This isn't all bad. If the wads of cotton candy collide with the popcorn in midair, we'll have sweet-and-salty kettle corn!

Kids are shrieking and ducking under tables for cover.

Except me. I can't really duck under anything anymore.

Ms. Denning's hair is glued to her face. She tried to put the plastic lid back on the cotton candy machine and took a direct sugar strand hit.

It's pure bedlam in the library. Forget about quiet, everybody is screaming!

Suddenly Coach Ball barges into the room.

He's brought Vice Principal Bumgarten and Gus, the janitor, with him.

Just the people we *don't* want to see.

Chapter 18

BATTLE OF THE BOOKS

What goes on here, Ms. Denning?" demands the principal.

"The school board's dreams came true!" I say, sounding as upbeat and positive as I can with popcorn kernels cotton-candy-glued to my cheeks. "Over half of the school population visited the library today!"

"Three hundred and fourteen students in thirty-two minutes," reports Pierce, who's running statistics for us.

"A very creative promotional idea," says Ms. Bumgarten, the vice principal who's all about the numbers.

"If by 'creative' you mean 'bad,'" snaps Coach Ball.

"Yes, sir," says Ms. Bumgarten, totally caving. "That's what I meant, sir. Bad, bad, bad!"

"But it worked," I say.

"So that's one for our team!" adds Gaynor, pumping his arm in victory. "Woo-hoo! USA! USA!"

"The library is saved!" adds Gilda.

"No, it is not," says Coach Ball, who's totally not joining in on the whole celebratory vibe in the room. "The only results that count are how many kids are using this library at the end of the month."

"We're not going for an average?" asks Pierce.

"No. I had a chat with Mrs. Lexi Critchett. She'll be back in twenty-two days to see how many kids are in the library."

"I'll be in charge of monitoring the statistics," says Ms. Bumgarten.

"Maybe," says Coach Ball.

"Right. Maybe." Ms. Bumgarten tries to smile. "Well, I have to run. Actually, I will walk, since running in the halls is against the rules...."

She leaves. Coach Ball turns his attention to Ms. Denning. "Now then—whose idea was this cheap popcorn-and-cotton-candy stunt?"

I raise my hand. "Me. It was sort of a bake sale.

Except we gave stuff away for free. And there weren't any cakes, cookies, or, you know, other baked goods."

"It was also sort of a mistake," says Ms. Denning. "A library doesn't need circus snacks to make it interesting, Jamie."

"Neither does a circus," says Gaynor. "But, whoa, they sure are tasty." He plucks a sugar-coated popcorn ball out of his hair.

"Our custodial staff is going to need to work overtime to clean this mess up," says Coach Ball.

"Might be best if we toss all these books in a dishwasher," suggests Gus, the janitor, pulling the walkie-talkie off his belt. "Gertie? This is Gus. When you're done washing the lunch dishes, have I got a job for you. And it's a doozy...."

"We can't clean books in a cafeteria dishwasher," says Ms. Denning, picking up a paperback. "That would ruin them!"

She can't open the book she's holding. The cover is glued to the pages with sugar.

I tug at my collar. "We, uh, might need to replace a few books."

"And how do you suggest we do that?" says Coach

Ball, jabbing his fists onto his hips so he can bend at the waist and glare at me from closer range.

"Well, uh, I…hummina, hummina, hummina…"

(Three *hummina*s in a row is what the classic comedian Jackie Gleason would say whenever he couldn't talk his way out of a jam.)

"I asked you a question, Mr. Grimm. How do you suggest we 'replace' these damaged books?"

"You could buy new ones," says Gilda, trying to help me out.

"Oh, really? *Buy* them? And where do you suggest we find the money for that?" The principal shakes his head with disgust. "This library is worse than useless. It is a money pit. A budgetary sinkhole. A financial fiasco!"

"Oh, you don't have to worry about the money, sir," I say.

"Oh, yes I do. I am the principal. Worrying about money is my job."

"I'm sorry. That's not what I meant. *You* don't have to worry about finding the money to replace the books because, uh, I will."

"Is that so?" Now Coach Ball leans back and grins. "Tell me more."

Chapter 19

"I'M DOING WHAT?"

I'm about to say hummina three times in a row again.

Luckily, Gilda jumps in and saves me.

"Jamie and his comedian friends are going to host a library benefit show."

"I am?"

Gilda nods like crazy.

"I mean, I *am!* I'm inviting all my comedian friends. We'll put on a show, sell tickets, maybe run a charity auction...."

"We could raffle off some props from *Jamie Funnie!*" says Gilda.

"Like that popcorn popper over there and the cotton candy machine, too," suggests Gaynor, trying to be helpful. He isn't. But like I said, he's trying.

Meanwhile, Gilda sort of oversells my ability to attract big-name comedians.

"Jamie knows everybody!" she says. "Chris Rock! Louis C.K.! Tina Fey! Ellen DeGeneres! Steven Wright! That guy from the *Mall Cop* movies..."

I like Gilda's idea, so I run with it. "We'll raise all the money the school needs to replace any damaged books and enough to buy some new ones, too!"

"I want that one about the robots who all live

together," says Gaynor. "I read the first two. They were incredibly cool."

"We might even raise enough to buy all the other cool stuff that Ms. Denning wants, like a 3-D printer," I say as she beams a big smile at me.

"I am not turning this school into one of your comedy nightclubs, young man," snarls Coach Ball.

"That's the best part," I tell him. "We're going to do the show at Long Beach's favorite dining spot: Good Eats by the Sea."

"But the school will receive all the proceeds," adds Pierce.

Coach Ball raises a skeptical eyebrow. "Will the owner of this 'Good Eats by the Sea' allow you to take over his establishment?"

"Oh, yes," says Ms. Denning. "He is a very good friend of the school library."

Friend?

He may just be friends with the library, but I know for sure that he's crazy about its librarian!

"Hey," I say, "while we're at it, we could raise enough money to buy your new wrestling team some more of those padded earmuffs."

Coach Ball narrows his eyes. "We don't need

your charity, Grimm. On my watch, sports teams at this school will always receive all the funding they require. That's how we create true Minnow pride—with proud new additions to the trophy case in the lobby." He turns to the janitor. "Come on, Gus. You can leave this mess until later. It's not like anybody's going to use the library now that all the popcorn and cotton candy are gone."

Coach Ball stomps out of the room. Gus sort of shuffles after him.

When they're gone, Ms. Denning turns to us.

"Look, you guys. I appreciate everything you're trying to do—especially the benefit show. That's a great idea. We can raise money and awareness at the same time. But I don't think we should try any more of these publicity stunts to draw kids into the library. I want kids to come here because they *want* to be here—not because there's free popcorn and cotton candy."

"What about cupcakes?" asks Gaynor. "Cupcakes would be huge."

Ms. Denning smiles. "Joey, I want kids to come to their library to learn and explore—not to grab a snack. You know, before I took this job, I worked at a public library. We had classes about everything, and they always drew a crowd."

"But this is a school, Ms. Denning," says Gilda. "Everybody takes classes all day long."

"That's why we have to make sure our after-school classes are fun!" says Ms. Denning.

Then she turns to me.

"Maybe even funny. If we had the right teacher."

Uh-oh.

Why do I have the feeling I'm about to involuntarily volunteer for something?

Chapter 20

LOVE IS FUNNY (AS IN WEIRD)

After the final bell, Gilda and I head down the boardwalk to Uncle Frankie's diner.

"So, are you going to teach one of those classes at the library?" asks Gilda. "Because if you do, I might, too."

"I have a better idea," I say. "Why don't you teach my class for me? You know as much about comedy as I do."

"Sure," she says. "The history and junk. But I don't know anything about doing stand-up comedy."

"Neither do I," I joke. "The whole standing part. I prefer to sit down on the job."

"You know what I mean. I could talk about classic comedy movies. Charlie Chaplin, the Marx

Brothers, the Three Stooges, the Three Amigos. But I couldn't help kids put together a comedy routine of their own."

"You've always helped me," I say, because Gilda's always been an excellent coach and sounding board. I'm always bouncing ideas off her. She has the lumps and bumps to prove it. "You'd be great teaching Funny Stuff 101."

"No, thanks, it's not really my thing," she says. "You should do it. Just think of all the kids you'll pull into the library." Her eyes light up. I can tell: She is having another one of her famous brainstorms. "Oh, oh. This is so awesome. You could schedule your class so it ends with a big showcase performance!"

I figure out where she's going with this. "On the day Mrs. Lexi Critchett and the rest of the school board will be coming back to see how many kids are in the library?"

"Exactly. You do the show at lunchtime and *boom!* The library is saved."

"I guess...."

"Look," says Gilda, "you concentrate on putting together your after-school lesson plans. I'll take charge of organizing the Stand Up for Books benefit show to raise money for the new library books. I'll call Jacky Hart at *Saturday Night Live* and ask her to help me book the talent."

"Deal."

"You really think Uncle Frankie will let us use his diner?" asks Gilda.

"Are you kidding? He'll do anything to save the library. He's cuckoo-nutso about Ms. Denning." I check my watch. "Ooops. I'm late. I'm on napkin-folding duty tonight."

"You guys are folding paper napkins now?"

"Uh-uh. We're all cloth all the time now. It's classier. And tonight, Uncle Frankie wants them to look like swans."

When we get to the diner, I notice that Uncle Frankie has changed the sign out front.

Good Eats by the Sea is now Culinary Excellence Near an Aquatic Setting.

We hurry into the restaurant.

I hardly recognize the place. The lights are sort of dim. The jukebox sounds like a late-night TV commercial for every sappy love song ever recorded.

And Uncle Frankie is wearing a tuxedo with tails and a top hat!

"Um, you know, Uncle Frankie," I say, "I'm not an expert on romance…"

"Tell me about it," says Gilda with an exaggerated eye roll.

I try to ignore that. "But, well, I'm not sure Ms. Denning is going to love the new you. Or the new diner."

"Are you kidding? She's a librarian. Librarians like elegant and tasteful stuff. Oh, listen to this. I memorized a poem today. It's librarian gold. Shows off my romantic side *and* my research skills. 'Roses are red, / that much is true. / But violets are violet, / and purple ain't blue.'"

That's when Ms. Denning comes into the diner. She looks around the dimly lit room.

"Oh, I'm sorry," she mumbles. "I must be in the wrong place."

And she's gone.

Gilda looks at me.

I look at Gilda.

Great. Now we have another after-school class to teach: Remedial Romance for Uncles.

Chapter 21

THE BOOK OF YUKS

The next day, I roll into the library during study hall.

If I'm going to teach a class on how to be funny, I realize I need to do some research and put together a lesson plan.

Turns out teachers have more homework than students. In fact, some of their homework is coming up with ideas for OUR homework! So if you think becoming a teacher means you only have to work till two or three in the afternoon, think again.

I'm clacking keys on a computer terminal, doing a search through the library's books, when Vincent O'Neil pops into the library.

"Hiya, Jamie."

The Secret Life of Teachers at Home

"Hey, Vincent."

He gestures toward the computer. "You know, a computer once beat me at chess. But it didn't stand a chance at kickboxing. Then there was the spider who crawled in here to use the computer. He wanted to check out his website."

"Um, I'm kind of busy right now," I say as nicely as I can.

"Really? What are you working on? New ideas for your *Jamie Funnie* TV show? Because I have a bunch. Like, for instance, you go bowling, but your fingers won't slip out of the ball, so you roll down the alley and score a strike."

"That's pretty good," I say. "But right now Gilda and I are working on something more important: saving the library."

"Ooh! Cool. Do you need any help coming up with ideas for that, too?"

"Sure. The more the merrier."

Vincent shoots me double finger pistols. "Excellent. Let me put it into the ol' brain hopper, see what hops out. Back in a flash!" He bustles out of the library.

I jot down a few call numbers and hit the

stacks. I load my lap up with a mound of comedy
books: Steve Martin's *Born Standing Up,* Tina
Fey's *Bossypants,* Jim Gaffigan's *Dad Is Fat,* Amy
Poehler's *Yes Please,* even a book called *Poo on You:
The World's Best Potty Jokes.*

I pile them all on a library table.

And then I just stare at them. I have no idea
what I am doing. Can I teach other kids to be stand-
up comics by reading them Jim Gaffigan jokes like
"You think when gym teachers are younger, they're
thinking, 'You know, I want to teach, but I don't
want to read'?"

"It looks as if you're studying hard," says Ms.
Denning.

"I'm going to go for it," I tell her, after pushing back from the table so we can make eye contact. "I'm going to teach an after-school class, right here in the library, on how to be a stand-up comic."

"That's fantastic. I anticipate that you will be a phenomenal pedagogue."

"Huh?"

"Sorry. I just started the library's Word of the Day bulletin board. If you can guess the meaning, you win a prize." She twiddles a pencil with an eraser-eater topper. It's a shark. It looks like it's about to devour a number two Ticonderoga. "*Pedagogue* is another word for *teacher*."

"Cool," I say, because I've just learned something.

And not just the meaning of a new word.

Nope, I have learned the secret to classroom success.

If you're going to be a teacher, a pedagogue, or even a pedant (another word for *teacher* I found because, hey, the library has a ginormous thesaurus), you've got to sound smart!

Super smart.

I need more books! The kind with big words!

Chapter 22

A DEGREE IN HEE-HEE-HEE

I roll back to the stacks.

This time I'm looking for all the comedic arts textbooks I can find. That's right, I'm talking *Theories of Humor and Laughter, Comedy's Impact on Twentieth-Century Culture,* and this really old book, *Laughter: An Essay on the Meaning of the Comic,* by some French dude who, I think, died before pie fights were even invented.

Yep. It's the kind of egghead stuff you'd read if you were a professor of laughology.

I pull out a notebook and start writing stuff down.

"In ancient Greece, comedy in the form of a play was one of the three principal dramatic forms."

That sounds smart.

I'm also wondering if Greek yogurt was as big in ancient Greece as it is in American supermarkets. And what makes it Greek if it's made in America? Guess it's a good thing they didn't call it yogurt of Greece. That just sounds oily.

But I digress.

I crack open another book and read a little of the *Laughter* essay.

"The comic does not exist outside the pale of what is strictly *human*....You may laugh at an animal, but only because you have detected in it some human attitude or expression."

Actually, I *never* laugh at animals. Many have fangs. Some are poisonous.

I reach a bunch of gobbledygook about the psychological significance of flatulence in humor. My eyelids get kind of heavy.

I yawn and move on to Shakespeare.

"Many of Shakespeare's most popular plays are comedies, such as his *Comedy of Errors*."

Okay. If it has *comedy* in the title, it has to be funny. Or maybe that was one of the errors?

My pen is kind of dragging across the page as I pry open another thick and dusty book.

"Stand-up comedy originated with court jesters in medieval times...."

The theory of comedy is making me sleepy. Very, very sleepy. I start daydreaming about what it would be like to be a court jester....

The next thing I know, my head's on the desk, someone is shouting, "Ms. Denning?" and I'm waking up in a pool of drool.

Yep, my lecture notes were so boring, I put myself to sleep.

"Ms. Denning?" booms the voice again. "This boy is using one of your books as a pillow!"

Uh-oh. It's the principal. Coach Ball!

He's sort of wagging his stubby finger at Ms. Denning.

"Just so we're clear on the rules, on the day of reckoning, students using this room for napping purposes will not count as students using the library. They must be awake."

He shows Ms. Denning a calendar page and pins it on the bulletin board over *pedagogue,* her Word of the Day.

The last day of the month is circled.

"You have three weeks to get more than fifty percent of the student body in here doing library stuff—not catching up on their beauty rest."

"Jamie was doing research," Ms. Denning tries to explain.

"Really? What was he studying? How to get a good night's sleep in the middle of the day?"

I try to joke my way out of another jam.

"You know, Coach Ball, that's funny. You remind me of something the great comic Steven Wright once said. Someone asked him, 'Did you sleep well?' He said, 'No, I made a couple of mistakes.'"

Ms. Denning chuckles.

Coach Ball basically growls.

He stomps out of the room. I look at my so-called lesson plan and reread the nonblurry parts where I didn't smear the ink with my snooze slobber.

Yep. It's just as boring the second time through.

Who am I kidding?

My class isn't going to be about comedy. It's going to be a tragedy.

Chapter 23

HEARD ANY BAD IDEAS LATELY?

After school, Gilda joins me in the library.

She's put together some terrific ideas for the Stand Up for Books benefit. We're all set to share them with Ms. Denning when Vincent O'Neil barges into the room.

"Prepare to be amazed!" he announces. "Your library is saved! I have come up with the best ideas ever!"

"Just as long as they aren't more publicity stunts," says Ms. Denning.

"Stunts?" says Vincent. "No way. These ideas are too huge to be called stunts."

"Great."

"Okay," he says, "there's this kids' book about a

lion who goes to the library for story hour. The kids use him as a pillow, and he helps dust the shelves with his tail and stuff. *Boom!* We do the same thing. We borrow a lion from the zoo! Bring him in here, have him dust shelves. Instant library mascot!"

We all look at Vincent like he's crazy.

"You want to keep a man-eating predator in the library?" says Gilda.

"Okay, okay. I hear your concerns. You're worried about potential liability issues. Insurance rates. I get that. Moving on. Next brainstorm: a library cheerleading squad."

He gives us a little demonstration.

"Instead of pom-poms," he says, "these cheerleaders shake shredded books."

"Shredded books?" gasps Ms. Denning.

"Right. Bad idea. Moving on. Idea three. Saved the best for last. Jamie teaches an after-school class about how to be a stand-up comic. He takes care of the comedy, I handle all the standing up stuff."

"Perfect!" I say just to stop Vincent from spewing any more toxic ideas into the ozone. I worry about global warming.

Of course, that means I'm still going to need a lesson plan, but I'm willing to make that sacrifice just to keep Vincent from soaking us with more drivel from his brainstorms.

"And while Jamie's been busy prepping his class notes," says Gilda, "I've been putting together an all-star lineup for the benefit at Uncle Frankie's diner, I mean dine-*aire*. We're going for Jacky Hart from *Saturday Night Live*—"

"She's awesome!" gushes Vincent.

"Jim Gaffigan is also a friend of our show," says Gilda, checking her notes. "He played a very happy customer at the diner in episode seven."

"I'm going to reach out to Jim first thing tomorrow," says Gilda.

"He's awesome, too!" says Vincent.

"I also want to call some of the contestants from the Planet's Funniest Kid Comic Contest. Antony Guerrero, Rebecca and Rachel Klein, Ben Baccaro."

"I am so psyched!" says Vincent. "All my comedy heroes and Jamie, too!" He practically skips out of the library.

When he's gone, Ms. Denning gestures for Gilda and me to move a little closer.

"Can I ask you guys to make another phone call?" she whispers.

"To the authorities about Vincent?" I whisper back. "Don't worry. He's harmless. Just a little overenthusiastic."

"I'm not worried about Vincent," says Ms. Denning. "It's your uncle Frankie. He seems so... different. He hasn't yo-yoed for me in days. He even wants to know which opera is my favorite."

Gilda and I both gulp. "He asked you about *opera?*"

Ms. Denning nods.

Wow. Uncle Frankie is in worse shape than we thought.

Chapter 2¾

UNCLE FRANÇOIS

After school on Monday, Gilda and I head to the diner to grab a quick snack.

And to have a word with Uncle Frankie.

On the way, we pass Crazy Bob—the guy with the cardboard sign about the upcoming alien invasion.

"The Galaxatronians are on their way," he tells us. "They'll be here by next weekend. Be sure you pack your toothbrush and a clean pair of underwear, Jamie!"

"Will do," I tell him. "Thanks for the heads-up."

Gilda and I each toss a quarter into his cup and hurry along to the diner. Uncle Frankie greets us at the door.

He's wearing that bow tie again.

"Hiya, Uncle Frankie," I say.

"Please, James. Call me François. It's much more distinguished sounding, don't you think?"

"Hey, I have an idea," I tell Uncle Frankie. "How about you show us a new yo-yo trick? You can try it out on Gilda and me. Then, if it's any good, you can show it to Ms. Denning when she gets here."

"That's a great idea," says Gilda.

Uncle Frankie curls his nose like someone just ordered a double portion of liver and onions.

"A yo-yo trick? For Flora? Tut, tut. I'm surprised that you two would suggest such an uncouth, uncultured, and unsophisticated activity. Yo-yoing is beneath the dignity of an intellectual such as Flora."

"No, it's not," I tell him. "Remember the other day, when she didn't even recognize this place and left?"

Uncle Frankie (I mean François) pats me on the head. "When you're older, James, you'll understand. Now if you will excuse me, I must go whip up some tuna tartare!"

"What's that?" I ask.

"Raw fish," says Gilda. "Bait."

"Hardly," says Uncle Frankie. "It is a gourmet delicacy. Says so in this *Gourmet Delicacy* magazine I checked out from the public library." He heads into the kitchen to *not* cook fish.

I slip behind the counter and take up my usual spot behind the cash register. Gilda grabs a stool.

I look around the dining room. Most of the booths

and tables are empty. I see more candles and folded napkins than people. All the changes at the diner haven't been great for romance *or* business.

Our most loyal regular, the big, burly bear Mr. Burdzecki, watches Uncle Frankie disappear into the kitchen, then rushes over to the counter.

"Quick," he says in his thick Russian accent. "Tell me a joke, Jamie. Do not recite more poetry."

"But Uncle Frankie said—"

"Please. I am begging you. No more poetry! A joke!"

"Um, okay." I look around to make certain Uncle Frankie can't hear me. Mr. Burdzecki's favorite comic is Russian, a guy named Yakov Smirnoff, who was huge back in the 1970s and '80s. But I know only about six of his jokes, and I've told them all to Mr. Burdzecki before. So I just make something up.

"What do you call a Russian who's eaten too many baked beans?"

Mr. Burdzecki shrugs. "I do not know. What do you call him?"

"Vladimir Tootin!"

Mr. B. slaps his knee. "Jamie, you funny!"

"Thanks," I say.

"No. I mean this. You funny. Do not forget this. It is who you are. And your poetry? It is not so good as your funny."

And just like that, I know what I have to do.

I have to give Uncle Frankie the same pep talk he was always giving me back when I was competing in the Planet's Funniest Kid Comic Contest. Whenever I was trying to work joke-book jokes into my act, he'd sit me down (okay, I was already seated, but you get the point) and say, "You're always better when you make up your own material, Jamie. Just be who you are. Give us *your* slant on life."

Now it's my turn to school him.

Ms. Denning wants Uncle Frankie to be Uncle Frankie, not Chef François.

"Wish me luck," I say to Gilda.

And then I roll into the kitchen to have the Talk.

Chapter 25

TALKING THE TALK
(WITHOUT WALKING THE WALK)

Um, Uncle Frankie? Can we talk?"

He gets a worried look in his eye. "Sure, kiddo. What's up?"

"Well, I'm probably not the best one to be giving you romantic advice—"

"True," says Gilda, who is hanging out in the doorway, pretending like she's not totally eavesdropping on us.

"Come on in," I tell Gilda with a sigh. "I might need your help."

"For what?" asks Uncle Frankie.

"Telling you the truth."

Gilda comes into the kitchen.

"Grab a pickle tub," I tell her.

She sits down on a five-gallon plastic bucket. Uncle Frankie sits down on the one next to hers.

"So, what's this all about?" asks Uncle Frankie. "Do we need fresh candles in the dining room? More Mozart symphonies in the jukebox?"

"No," I say. "We need doo-wop music. And burgers. And fries with gravy."

"And napkins that don't look like frozen birds," adds Gilda.

"Oh. I get it. You kids aren't crazy about the improvements. Well, our more sophisticated clientele, such as the librarians of the neighborhood, enjoy the finer things in life, including properly folded napkins and flickering candelabras."

I shake my head. "No, they don't. They like yo-yos and you-you."

"Huh?"

"Ms. Denning," says Gilda. "She likes you for you, sir. The old you. The one in the white apron with the grease stains and ketchup splatters."

"It's like you always tell me, Uncle Frankie," I say. "It's always best to be yourself instead of some version of who you think other people want you to be."

Uncle Frankie smiles a little. "Flora wants me to yo-yo?"

I nod. "Yes!"

"She likes you for you," says Gilda. "As a guy, you probably have a hard time realizing that. Most guys never know when a girl is truly interested in them."

Gilda gives me a funny, eyebrows-raised look. I don't know why.

"She told you kids this?" asks Uncle Frankie, fiddling with his black bow tie.

"Yep," I say.

"I see," he says, looking like he's doing some serious thinking. After a moment, he jumps up and shouts, "Thank goodness!"

Gilda and I can only stare as he yanks off his tie and then peels open his formal monkey suit like Superman.

Gilda and I help Uncle Frankie blow out all the candles in the restaurant and turn up all the lights.

"Buh-bye, Mr. Mozart!" Uncle Frankie bops the side of the jukebox. A doo-wop group starts singing "Why Do Fools Fall in Love."

One line strikes me as extremely strange: "Why does the rain fall from up above?"

"Because it would be weird if rain came up out of the dirt," I want to tell the singer. But he's too busy rhyming *above* with *love*.

And that's when Ms. Denning comes through the door. She's beaming. Uncle Frankie is beaming and twirling his yo-yo. Fools are falling in love all over the place!

"Isn't this wonderful?" says Gilda, batting her eyes at me.

"Yeah," I tell her. "Now we can order a cheeseburger deluxe with cheesy fries again."

The way Gilda rolls her eyes at me tells me one thing.

That wasn't the answer she was going for.

Chapter 26

Comedy
for
Dunces

HAPPY DAYS ARE HERE AGAIN

Uncle Frankie is back to flipping burgers with one hand while twirling yo-yo tricks with the other.

"I call this little combo the Breakaway Pinwheel Lindy Loop with a Time-Warp Twist!" he says, showing off his flashy moves to Ms. Denning.

Notice how my hands never leave my arms!

Ms. Denning is thrilled.

"Now this is the Francis I..."

Whatever she was about to say, she changes it in midsentence.

"Remember."

Ms. Denning becomes even happier when Pierce and Gaynor show up with the poster they've been putting together for the Stand Up for Books benefit this coming Friday night.

"You really got Jacky Hart *and* Jim Gaffigan?" She sounds amazed.

"Yep," says Gilda. "Gaffigan *loves* food. Told me a diner is his idea of what heaven will be like. Especially if there's pie."

"Oh, there will be," says Uncle Frankie. "Apple, cherry, and banana cream!"

"Those dudes from the funny-kid competition are coming, too," says Gaynor, tapping their names on the poster.

"Antony Guerrero, the Klein sisters, and Ben Baccaro all said yes," adds Pierce.

"And of course," says Gilda, "Jamie is the headliner. The big draw. The hometown hero. The one everybody is coming to see, live and in person."

Gulp.

I wish she hadn't put it that way. Did I mention that I have a bad habit of panicking right before my biggest shows? You could write a book about it. Maybe even five.

As everybody else has a great dinner of meat loaf, peas, and mashed potatoes, I can feel the flop sweat dribbling down my back like rain gushing out of a leaf-clogged gutter.

That night, things go from bad to worse to horrible.

The aliens land!

Yep. Crazy Bob was right.

The Galaxatronians arrive early. Around midnight. They blast the boardwalk, demolish the diner, and totally scorch the school. On the plus side, since we don't have a school *or* a library anymore, I don't have to worry about prepping a lesson plan for that class on how to be a comedian.

Too bad I wake up and realize the world hasn't come to an end. It was just another one of my wacky nightmares. I guess it comes from falling asleep worrying about all the scary stuff: the benefit, the comedy class, and the fact that Stevie Kosgrov sleeps two doors down.

The next morning, I roll into the library and talk to Ms. Denning.

"I think I have to focus on the benefit show this week," I tell her. "When that's done, I'll put together my plans for the comedy class." I gesture toward the calendar, where the last day of the month is circled in red. "We'll still have two whole weeks to pack the library with kids for the big day at the end of the month."

"That sounds like an excellent idea," she says. "I bet we can sign up a ton of students for your class at the benefit concert! Plus, with you, Jacky Hart, and Jim Gaffigan, who knows—we might raise enough money to buy more books, more computers, more iPads, and a 3-D printer for our new makerspace! If we have those things, that'll be sure to draw more kids to the library, too. No pressure, though."

Outside, I'm smiling and nodding.

Inside? I'm sweating and dying!

Chapter 27

BRAINSTORMS WITH A CHANCE OF FOG

I realize that what I need (besides a bus ticket out of town) is some brand-new material for the benefit show.

So after school, Gilda, Pierce, Gaynor, and I meet in the library to work up a fresh routine.

"Okay," says Gilda, "it's a benefit for the school library...."

"So just do a string of library jokes, dude," says Gaynor. "Duh. That was easy."

"Well done," says Pierce. He and Gaynor knock knuckles.

Then they look at me.

"Um, okay, uh…" I rack my brain, trying to remember any library jokes I might've read or heard. "Okay. Here's one. A guy comes into the library with an overdue book. The librarian says, 'This book about amnesia was due four weeks ago!' The guy says, 'Really? I forgot.'"

Gaynor chuckles. Pierce grimaces. Gilda shakes her head.

And that's when Vincent O'Neil barges into the room.

"Hi, guys. Is this another brainstorming session?"

"Yes," I tell him. "I need new material for the Stand Up for Books show…*this Friday night!* It's like three days away because it *is* three days away!"

I'm pretty sure everyone can hear the panic in my voice.

"Well," says Vincent, "since it's a benefit for a library, you should do library and librarian jokes!"

"That's what I said!" exclaims Gaynor. "Total no-brainer, dude."

"However," says Pierce, "it might be best if they were *good* jokes."

"No problemo!" says Vincent. "I've got a million of 'em! Do you know where librarians sleep?

Between the covers. When they eat dinner, they use bookplates. If you go to a seven-story library and check out seven books, how many are left? None! I told you they had only seven stories!"

My favorite books? *Parachuting*, by Hugo First.

Mosquito Bites, by Ivan Itch.

Why Cars Stop, by M.T. Tank.

And, of course, the classic, *Under the Bleachers*, by I. Seymour Butts.

"O-kay," says Gilda when Vincent finishes his run of one-liners. And then she gets that look in her eye again. The one where you can actually see the brainstorm clouds swirling madly inside her brain. "Oooh. I've got it. This is fabtastic. You don't write any material!"

"What?"

143

"You do an improv. An off-the-cuff, seat-of-your-pants, no-prep book talk!"

"Huh?"

Gilda hops up and grabs a library cart loaded down with books that Ms. Denning plans on reshelving.

"Close your eyes and pick one," she tells me. "And then tell me about it."

I give it a shot. What do I have to lose?

The first book I pluck off the cart is *The Maze Runner,* by James Dashner.

"Ah, yes," I say. "One of my favorites. It's all about a mouse in a twisted psychology experiment who can't find the cheese in a maze, so he keeps running around." I do a rodent face and a squeaky mouse voice. "Where's my cheese? Come to think of it, where are my Cheetos? Where's the nearest Chuck E. Cheese's? It's my birthday!"

Everybody cracks up.

Gilda tosses me another book.

"Harry Potter and the Sorcerer's Stone," I say, reading the title. And then I wing another book talk. "This is all about a very hairy guy who likes to make pottery. He has one of those wheels and all

sorts of wet clay, but every time he goes to throw a bowl, his hair gets tangled up in the spinning mud." I grab my throat like my long locks have become a noose around my neck. "Ack! It's dangerous being a hairy potter...."

"Hysterical!" declares Gilda.

"Awesome," adds Gaynor.

"Very amusing," says Pierce.

"And," says Vincent, "if you run out of ideas, you can always use some of my librarian jokes."

"Thanks," I say.

But I don't think I'm going to need any of Vincent's material. Thanks to Gilda, I feel funny again!

Chapter 28

ROLLING ON
THE FLOOR LAUGHING

Friday night, the diner is packed.

It's standing room only for everybody except me and a few of my wheelchair buds.

Uncle Frankie is in his tuxedo (but he's not saying "Tut, tut" or calling himself François anymore) giving everybody the red carpet treatment as they enter. Ms. Denning shows up wearing a sparkly gown. I think she made it with a glue gun and sequins in her new makerspace at the library. The Smileys are there, too. Fortunately, Stevie isn't with them. I spy the new principal, Coach Ball, lurking in the shadows near the jukebox. He's chugging some kind of goopy protein shake out of a plastic bottle. And belching.

Then Jacky Hart comes in with some of her castmates from *Saturday Night Live*. Jim Gaffigan is right behind her, and the crowd goes crazy.

"Welcome, everybody," I say, since I'm the emcee, or master of ceremonies. "Thank you all for being here tonight and helping us raise so much money for the Long Beach Middle School library!"

The crowd applauds.

"We hope to have you all rolling on the floor with laughter...not just me and my pals in the wheelchairs. And don't forget to bid on all the cool stuff in the silent auction. Jacky Hart has donated an autographed copy of her book, *Jacky Ha-Ha*. I signed a copy of the first *Jamie Funnie* TV show script. And Mr. Gaffigan signed a sandwich he didn't finish for lunch today."

Gaffigan leans down and takes my mic. "Do you know how hard it is to sign your name in mustard and ketchup?" he jokes.

We start the show with some hilarious routines from my pals from the Planet's Funniest Kid Comic Contest.

Ben and the Klein sisters are hysterical, like always. But Antony Guerrero, who was the Southwest Regionals winner from Albuquerque, New Mexico, does a killer set that slays everybody.

(Nobody really died—that's just what we say when a comedian is amazing!)

You know, I would've been onstage sooner, but some nice folks outside kept asking me to rake their leaves and mow their lawn.

Yes, I am Hispanic. That means my family lived in New Mexico back when it was just, you know, Mexico!

I understand that some people want to build a wall on the border between the United States and Mexico. I'm not sure it's going to work. Why? One word: tunnels.

I've always admired Antony's comedy. He's fearless and never worries about being politically correct.

After he finishes, Jacky Hart takes the stage with a few of her *Saturday Night Live* friends.

Since we're in a diner doing a benefit for a literary cause, they do a funny sketch about Shakespeare's *Hamelet*—a play all about a ham and Swiss omelet.

It's pretty funny. Especially when Jacky and her friends do modern dance moves, pretending to be the sizzling, shriveling ham.

Gilda wheels in a library cart loaded down with books. "You're up after Gaffigan," she reminds me.

Not that she has to.

I'm sweating more than that fried ham in Jacky Ha-Ha's *Hamelet*.

Especially when I notice who just slipped into the diner: Stevie Kosgrov and Lars Johannsen!

Chapter 29

BACKSTAGE HORROR SHOW

I roll into the kitchen, which we've sort of turned into a greenroom (the place where performers wait before going onstage).

It's a good place to focus on getting ready to do my improv routine. It's also an excellent location for hiding from Stevie and Lars.

Or so I thought.

"Whatcha doin' back here, funny boy?" snarls Lars as he and Stevie stride into the kitchen.

"What a coincidence," says Stevie. "This is where his uncle Frankie stores all the dead meat."

"No," I say. "Actually, the meat goes into the walk-in refrigerator."

"Great," says Lars. "That's where Coach says we

should put you. In deep freeze."

"Coach said that?" I gasp. "He's the school principal!"

Stevie and Lars just grin and grab my armrests.

"The freezer is this way," says Stevie. "I sneak in here and steal frozen hot dogs all the time. I love me a meaty Popsicle."

"Is that so?" says a voice I'm very glad to hear. Uncle Frankie. "I thought that was some other giant rat. What are you two boys doing back here?"

"Nothin'," grunts Lars.

"We just came to see the show," adds Stevie. "It's a free country."

"Not tonight," says Uncle Frankie. "This is a benefit show. Tickets start at fifty bucks. If you want to be this close to the talent, it'll cost you *five hundred*." He holds out his hand.

"Um, we gotta go," says Stevie.

"Yeah," says Lars. "I hear my mother calling me."

"Is that what that is?" I say, holding my hand to my ear. "I thought it was a moose."

Lars balls up his fist. Uncle Frankie steps forward.

"You don't want to keep your mommy waiting," he tells Lars.

Stevie and Lars leave—but not without trying to get in the last word: "This isn't over, Gimp!"

"They're right," says Uncle Frankie. "It's not over until you go on! Come on, kiddo."

"Thanks," I say. "For everything."

He gives me a smile, a wink, and a head rub. "Right back at ya! Flora was so excited by the big turnout, she gave me a kiss on the cheek!"

We head out just in time to catch the end of Gaffigan's set.

He wraps up his foodie routine by saying, "I wish every comedy club were a diner. That way, when I tell jokes about bacon, I could eat it at the same time! Thank you, everybody. Support the library. Help my pal Jamie Grimm help his school. And send me all your bacon! And now, ladies and gentlemen, put your hands together for the one and only Jamie Grimm!"

Yep. It's my turn.

I freeze for a second. I can't remember any of my jokes.

Then I remember: I'm not doing any jokes! I'm improvising. Making stuff up on the fly.

It sounded like such a good idea when Gilda suggested it.

But that was back before I actually had to do it.

What was I thinking?

Chapter 30

BOOKING IT!

I roll into the spotlight.

Jim Gaffigan hands me the mic.

"Have fun," he says. "I'm going into the kitchen to make a bacon, lettuce, and bacon sandwich, hold the lettuce."

"Ladies and gentlemen, Jim Gaffigan!" I say, reaching a hand in his direction.

Everyone applauds.

Then I ask for another round of applause for "all the terrific comedians who volunteered their time to be here tonight to help us raise funds for the Long Beach Middle School library. None of them are getting paid—"

"We're not?" cracks Ben Baccaro, the comic who

calls himself the Italian Scallion. He always wears a tight white tee that shows off his bulging chest muscles, and wiggles them every time he cracks a joke.

"How am I going to pay for this meatball sub?" he jokes.

"It's on me!" says Uncle Frankie.

"I know. I've seen your apron! Bada bing!"

The crowd cracks up. Everybody's having such a great time, their energy gets my comedy juices flowing.

"So," I say, "since this is a benefit for the library, I thought I'd book-talk a few titles."

Gilda pushes a library cart into my spotlight. It's loaded with books I haven't seen yet.

Yep. I'm going to do this crazy trapeze act without a net.

"What do we have here? Ah, yes. *Charlotte's Web.* All about the terrible Internet service in a city in North Carolina. Don't know why there's a pig on the cover."

"Bacon!" shouts Jim Gaffigan from off stage.

Another wave of laughter washes over me. I dive in!

The bit works so well, I have to give Gilda a huge hug when I'm done.

"You were fantastic!" she tells me.

"If I was," I say, "it was all thanks to you!"

She grabs the microphone out of my lap. "Hey, you guys?" she says to the crowd. "Major announcement. Starting next week, right after school, Jamie Grimm, this funny guy right here, will be in the library teaching a class on how to become a comedian. And at the end of the course, in two weeks, the best comics in the class will put on a show, just like this one, in the library. If you're interested, there's a sign-up sheet over there on that table. See you on Monday in the library!"

All the kids in the crowd rush the table.

"Um, how many slots do we have for students?" I ask Gilda.

"As many as sign up! Maybe the whole school!"

Mrs. Smiley, who works at a bank, volunteered to handle all the money for the benefit. When she comes over and tells us how much we've raised from tickets and all the silent auction items, Ms. Denning nearly faints.

"That's enough to do everything we dreamed about doing!" She gives me a hug.

Uncle Frankie? He gets another kiss!

"Congrats, Jamie," says Jacky Hart, coming over to shake my hand. "You done good, kiddo."

"Thanks," I tell her. "But, well, I had the best do-gooding teacher!"

I gesture toward Uncle Frankie, who's busy making goo-goo eyes at Ms. Denning.

"So, Flora," I hear him say, "guess this means you'll be sticking around a little longer, huh?"

"I sure hope so, Francis."

I'm feeling pretty great. And then Coach Ball comes over to rain on my parade.

"Nice crowd," he says, his face scrunched up like he has more gas than Vladimir Tootin guzzling British vinegar. "Too bad this doesn't count. The crowd the school board is interested in has to be in the library, Grimm, not at a diner listening to smart-aleck celebrities crack jokes. We'll see how many kids are using Ms. Denning's book boneyard at the end of the month. Never forget, Grimm—it's *my* school. I make all the rules."

Chapter 31

FIRST-CLASS TREATMENT?

Monday morning at the middle school, almost the entire student body signs up for my first How to Do Stand-Up class.

Everybody had so much fun watching the show that they want to be *in* the next show! Gilda and Ms. Denning are taking names at a table they've set up in the hallway outside the library.

"Join us right after school," announces Gilda during the shuffle between first and second periods. "A special library-only class taught by the Planet's Funniest Kid Comic and star of the hit TV series *Jamie Funnie,* Jamie Grimm himself!"

"This is going to be so awesome!" I hear one kid

say as she writes her name on Ms. Denning's yellow legal pad.

"I want my own TV show, too!" says another.

"I was born to be funny," says a third. "And make money from it!"

"Sign on up!" says Gilda, in full carnival-barker mode. "Learn how to do stand-up!"

"Maybe I should take this class," I joke to Gilda. "I'd love to learn how to stand up again."

She laughs it off, but I'm sweating bullets. It's what I always do when the pressure is on. Which it is.

Constantly.

For me, life is one giant pressure cooker with the lid locked down tight.

I perspire my way through the rest of the day. I feel sorry for everybody who has to sit behind me. I would also like to publicly apologize to Gus, the janitor.

The final bell rings at 2:40.

I'm in the library by 2:48. I might've made it there sooner, but I had to fight my way through the mob of kids heading toward the library. To take my class!

It's standing room only. About a dozen kids are out in the hallway because the vice principal, Ms. Bumgarten, says we've reached the fire marshal's safe occupancy limit.

"Well done," she says, looking around to make sure Coach Ball isn't lurking in the shadows.

"Well, if we need more room, I could wait out in the hall, too," I suggest.

Ms. Bumgarten grins. Ms. Denning laughs.

They both think I'm joking.

I'm not.

I'm panicking!

"Too bad the school board isn't here today," says Ms. Denning. "We'd save the library for sure."

Save the library, I tell myself. *For the school. For the other kids. For Uncle Frankie. For LOVE!*

This is it. I've got to do this thing! I'm on.

"Um, good afternoon, everybody. I'm Jamie Grimm. Rhymes with *fwschlimm*." Everyone chuckles. So I keep going, even though my voice is sort of shaky. "It also rhymes with *him*. And *hymn*. You know, the one that's a song, not a person. 'Amazing Grace'…"

O-kay.

No one's laughing anymore. Now they're just sort of staring. Bewilderment, I think they call it.

Meanwhile, I'm hearing crickets. The biology lab is right across the corridor, and we're doing a unit on tracking cricket population growth. It's much more interesting than *my* class!

"Um, thanks for coming here to the library, which, um, is where we are right now. But you probably knew that, since you came to the, uh, library to take this class. Soooo. I'm really excited to be here, in the library, to talk to you all about the art of comedy, in the library."

Then my mind goes blank. It's as blank as a… something. Something with nothing on it. Yes, my mind is so blank, I can't even make a metaphor anymore.

I try to remember some of that research I did about the art of comedy.

"A wise person once said that comedy equals tragedy plus time."

"What is this, Jamie?" hollers Vincent O'Neil, who, of course, has a front-row seat. "Math class?"

He gets a laugh.

I get a little wetter under my armpits.

"Ha, ha," I say. "Very funny, Vincent. Yes, success as a stand-up comic is a goal desired by many and achieved by few. And yet, with the proper combination of determination, research, and practice, you, too, can fulfill your dreams."

Maybe I shouldn't have mentioned dreams. Maybe I shouldn't talk and gesture like I'm a stiff in a late-night TV commercial for the Acme Truck Driving School. I'm so boring, people are starting to nod off. My after-school class is turning into pre-K nap time.

"Some of the best comedy ever created deals with painful subjects," I say, my voice squeaking. "A comedian named David Steinberg once said something like, if you don't have problems, you're going to be a lousy comedian. In other words, you have to suffer to be funny."

"Well, I'm definitely suffering right now," cracks Vincent.

So am I.

I not funny.

I the worst thing in the world.

I *boring*.

Chapter 32

CHICKEN FOR LUNCH

Tuesday, I make the smartest move of my entire teaching career: I postpone my class!

"Principal—I mean *Coach* Ball wants a big turnout in the gym after school for his first wrestling team exhibition match," I explain to the gang over lunch in the cafeteria. "I think it's very important that we all be there to show our school spirit and, you know, Fighting Minnow pride!"

"*Bruck, bruck, bruuuck,*" says Gaynor, tucking his thumbs under his pits and flapping his elbows.

"Are you implying that Jamie is chicken?" says Pierce. "That he is afraid to face his after-hours pupils again following yesterday's fiasco?"

"No," cracks Gilda. "Gaynor's just doing his

imitation of our delicious cafeteria food. Hey, Jamie, remember when you used to do jokes about our oh-so-tasty lunches?" She jiggles her plate. Her rubbery chicken nuggets bounce around and dance.

"No. Not really."

"I do."

"You sure you don't want to teach my comedy class for me?" I ask her. "You do me better than I did me yesterday."

"You had one bad afternoon," Gilda replies with a shrug. "It happens. But I'll tell you what I *will* do."

"What?"

"Go with you to the wrestling dealio this afternoon!"

"It's a date!" I say.

"Ooooh," snigger Gaynor and Pierce. "A daaaaate."

Gilda is beaming.

Me? I'm wishing I used a different word. I'm also sweating again. Profusely. Poor Gus. He's going to need to mop up the cafeteria floor, too.

Chapter 33

I WANT TO HOLD YOUR HAND

After school, Gilda and I head to the gym together.

Since it's a "date," I'm wondering if I should hold her hand. Too bad I can't. I need both my hands to pump my wheels—otherwise our whole date would just be me turning around in a circle.

We take our usual floor seats.

There's a big wrestling mat done up in our school colors occupying half of the gym floor. Coach Ball is in the center with his microphone, standing on a big picture of our school mascot, the minnow. Except it's a new version I haven't seen before—now it's a very angry fish. Next to it is a big ad for Meathead protein shakes, whatever those are.

On one side of the thick foam mat, I see Stevie and Lars decked out in snarling-minnow wrestling gear. On the other side are two kids, about half their size, from Valley Stream Middle School.

"Thank you all for coming out this afternoon to support our newest team," says Coach Ball. "Our heavyweights are made even heavier by Meathead protein shakes. Prepare to be amazed!"

Well, I certainly am.

The whole exhibition lasts about three minutes.

Lars pins his guy in fifteen seconds. The crowd in the bleachers goes wild! The cheerleaders break into a very special cheer they must've just made up.

"Lars!" *Clap-clap.* "He is ours!" *Clap-clap.* "He's so large." *Clap-clap.* "Looks like a barge!" *Clap-clap.*

"I am triumphant!" declares Lars as he struts around the ring, both fists raised high above his head. "I am invincible!"

Stevie takes a little longer to defeat his opponent, but he puts on more of a show.

He uses some of his schoolyard bully techniques to give the kid from Valley Stream a wrestling-uniform wedgie, before doing the old behind-the-ankle trip to lay him out flat on his back. Then Stevie just sits on the poor guy's chest while the ref does the two-count for the pin.

"There you have it!" booms Coach Ball through his microphone. "An early glimpse at what promises to be the first of many championship seasons for the Long Beach Middle School wrestling team."

Then he turns to me and Gilda.

"Just think how much more awesome this

school's team would be if they had a real sweat room to work out in."

Then he does that double-fingers-to-his-eyes-to-me-to-his-eyes bit again.

Oh, yeah.

He wants our library. He wants it bad.

Chapter 34

ROUND TWO

Realizing that Coach Ball is gunning for the library and that time is not exactly on our side, I come back to school on Wednesday with a renewed sense of purpose.

I also renew a book in the library because I didn't get a chance to finish it. I was too busy worrying about flopping, and watching Stevie sit on people, to read much more than the table of contents.

But on the way home from the wrestling match, Gilda gives me a good talking to.

"You need to snap out of your funk, Jamie," she says. "We're all counting on you. We have eight school days left to pack the library, or we'll both be helping Ms. Denning pack up all the books!"

And so at 2:40, when that final bell rings, I grit my teeth and roll back to the library, ready to rock the school of laughs!

Unbelievably, about 90 percent of my students are back for round two. They must really want to be comics. Either that or they really enjoy watching me crash and burn.

"Hi, guys," I say. "It's great to be back and to see so many of you back, too. I promise you a great class today, because during study hall I whipped up an awesome lesson plan!"

They applaud.

I reach for my backpack, which should be hanging on the back of my chair.

But it isn't.

Because I left it in my locker.

I have something in common with my students. None of us knows what I'm going to say next.

"Yo, loser!"

For the first time in my life, I am actually happy to see Stevie Kosgrov nearly knock a door off its hinges as he bursts it open and stomps into the library. Lars Johannsen isn't with him, but Stevie's brought his regular two minions, Zits and Useless. All three of them are chugging those Meathead protein shakes. And belching.

They're a nice distraction from how unprepared I am to teach this class.

Stevie plops down into a chair. "I heard your class stinks worse than your breath, Cornball. Thought I'd drop by to watch you die."

Dying is what comics call it when their jokes bomb and nobody in the audience is laughing.

I turn this disruption into a teachable moment.

"Stevie here is what we comedians call a heckler. That's a person in the audience who thinks he's funnier than the person on the stage. If you are going to be a stand-up comic, you need to be armed with snappy replies for any heckling situation. For instance, I could say to my heckler, 'Hey, I bet your brain feels good as new, seeing how you've never used it.'"

A few brave students laugh.

Stevie fakes a great big yawn.

"I heard you're the most boring teacher in the world," he says. "Now I know it's true. You're better than a sleeping pill!"

"You can also attempt to out-heckle the heckler," I explain to the class. I clear my throat and address Stevie directly.

"Oh, having trouble sleeping? What's the matter?" I switch into a funny goo-goo baby voice. "Did Mommy forget to pack your blankie, Binky, and baby bottle in your itty-bitty lunch box today?"

That earns me a little snicker, so I keep going.

"Can someone show Stevie where the library keeps the coloring books and crayons?"

Stevie stands up. No one is laughing anymore.

In fact, the way he's glaring at the crowd—he's daring them even to *think* about laughing again. Everyone looks terrified.

Not exactly the reaction I was hoping for in my comedy class.

Chapter 35

GIVING IN TO THE DARK SIDE

Stevie is not done heckling me.

"Your jokes are so lame," he says, "they're crippled. So they're just like you, Lamie Jamie."

He moves forward two steps. I start to seethe.

"You think you're funny?" Stevie says. "I do, too. Funny looking. Funny smelling. Funny as in *not normal and never will be*."

I have no more snappy comebacks. I am *mad*.

"You know what else?" Stevie sneers. "I bet your parents and little sister are super glad they're not here to see just how lame you turned out to be."

Forget the lesson plan. Forget everything.

Stevie knows I lost both my parents and my baby sister in a horrible car crash. The same horrible car crash that put me in my wheelchair. He knows I'd do anything to have them back.

"Jamie?" Gilda pleads. "Just ignore him."

I think that's what she says. All I hear is *whoosh-whoosh-whoosh* and *whump-whump-whump*.

Have you ever been so mad, so hurt, that the whole world slows down, and everything sounds sluggish and slurred, the way it does when you dunk your head underwater in the bathtub?

That's where I am. In a red zone of total rage.

Back when I was a rookie comic, I made a mistake making fun of my friends and family for a few cheap and easy laughs. After that, I made a vow: I would never do it again. I would never, *ever* be funny at the expense of people I cared about.

Back then I realized that if I lost my compassion, if I didn't care whom my comedy hurt, then I'd be no better than all the people who've ever hurt me.

But when Stevie made that crack about my mother and father and baby sister?

That whole vow flew right out the window.

In fact, I make a new vow: I will do whatever it takes, no matter the cost, to once and for all verbally rip Stevie Kosgrov to shreds.

I can't believe I'm becoming that guy. The insult comedian. The put-down comic. It's terrible. But I can't stop.

"These guys are so dumb, they need to study for a blood test. They couldn't pour water out of a bottle even if the instructions were on the bottom."

No one in the library is laughing. I think Gilda might actually be sobbing. Ms. Denning is calling someone on her phone. Everybody else looks extremely nervous.

Probably because they know what's coming next.

I figure I have time to hit Stevie with one last put-down before he puts *me* down on the floor.

"The other day, Stevie had to write a paper for school and asked me how to spell *TV*."

He socks me in the gut.

I topple backward and end up sprawled on my butt.

All I can see are stars. And stampeding feet.

Even though my sole purpose for teaching was to bring kids *into* the library, all my students are running *out*. They want to leave before Stevie turns on them.

"Class dismissed," I whisper.

But everyone is already gone.

Chapter 36

HAVING A FRANKIE DISCUSSION

Gaynor and Pierce help me back into my chair.

They do that a lot.

"You okay?" asks Pierce.

I force a smile and pat down my arms and chest. "Just fine. Nothing's broken that wasn't broken before."

"Dude," says Gaynor, "you went totally ballistic on Stevie's butt."

"I guess."

"You had the last punch line," Gilda says sadly. "But he got the last punch."

"He usually does," I remind her.

"Which is why you should just avoid him, Jamie."

"I do. I did! He's the one who came barging into

the library like he owned the place."

"Everyone is welcome in the library," says Ms. Denning, sliding her phone into her back pocket.

"Even big fat jerks and bullies?"

"They're our favorites," she says with a smile. "Because if bullies start reading about other people's experiences, they might lose some of their jerkiness. Reading—especially fiction—helps us walk a mile in someone else's shoes."

"I'd be happy to walk ten feet in my own sneakers," I mutter, because, yes, I am still feeling super sorry for myself. It happens.

"Hey, why don't you go see Uncle Frankie," suggests Ms. Denning. "I just gave him a call. He's expecting you."

"That's a great idea," says Gilda. "Let's all go grab a burger."

"It might be best if Jamie went alone," says the librarian.

"Oh," says Gaynor. "It's one of *those* 'go see Uncle Frankies.'…"

Pierce actually takes off his porkpie hat. "Good luck, Jamie," he says somberly.

"What is this?" I ask. "My funeral?"

"Maybe," says Gilda. "If so, what kind of flowers do you like?"

"The kind that squirt lemon juice in everybody's eyes."

Gilda cringes.

I roll out of the school building and take my time wheeling my way down the boardwalk to what I'm sure is going to be a major-league lecture from Uncle Frankie.

When I hit the diner, Uncle Frankie's waiting for me at the front door.

"Hiya, kiddo," he says. "How's your day been?"

"What? Didn't your girlfriend tell you when she called to rat me out?"

Uncle Frankie motions for me to join him at a booth.

"Flora did call me," he explained, "but only because she's worried about you. To tell you the truth, Jamie, I am, too. Why'd you lose your cool like that?"

"Because Stevie started saying incredibly nasty stuff about Mom and Dad and little Jenny."

"And you let it get to you?"

"Yes. I'm not made out of a nonstick surface like one of your frying pans."

"You know, Jamie, there's always a reason people like Stevie act the way they do."

"Because they're big fat jerks and that's just what big fat jerks do?"

Uncle Frankie smiles gently and places a hand on my shoulder.

"I talked to Stevie's mother the other day."

"Aunt Smiley?"

Frankie nods. "She came in for a bowl of clam chowder. Told me how hard it is for Stevie, you being famous and all. So now he's hooked up with your principal, this Coach Ball character. Stevie's trying to become a big-shot wrestler. Guzzling those horrible Meathead protein shakes to bulk up. Why? So he can be famous like you. Trouble is Coach Ball keeps riding Stevie's butt. Pushing him to do stuff he really doesn't want to do."

"You mean exercise? Run laps?"

"Worse," says Uncle Frankie. "He's making Stevie become meaner and angrier and more hateful than he's ever been before. A lot of it is aimed at you and Flora because the coach wants to get his grubby mitts on that library space. So all I'm saying, Jamie, is what some wise man said many moons ago: Be kind, because everyone you meet is fighting a hard battle you know nothing about."

"Even Stevie?"

Frankie nods. "Even Stevie."

"Oh, great. So now you're on his side?"

"No, Jamie. I'm just saying—"

"I know what you're saying, because you just said it!" I snap. "Thanks for the great advice. Now, if you'll excuse me, I need to go home and figure out some way to save your stupid girlfriend's job."

Yeah.

Stevie isn't the only one who can be a ginormous jerk.

Chapter 37

BATTLE TALK

Whenever I act lousy, I also feel lousy.

Which, of course, reminds me of a corny old Henny Youngman joke.

A man's not feeling good, so he goes to see his doctor. The doctor says, "Take your clothes off and stick your tongue out the window."

"What will that do to make me feel better?" asks the patient.

"Nothing," says the doctor, "but I'm mad at my neighbor!"

BA-DUM-CHING!

Anyway, instead of heading home to Smileyville, I retreat to the boardwalk and my bench. The sun is just starting to set. So it's not exactly nighttime, but I'm hoping that maybe Cool Girl will, once again, sense that I'm in trouble and she'll be there a little earlier than usual to help me cool down.

She isn't.

But Gilda is. Funny how that's been happening lately.

"What took you so long to get here?" she cracks.

"Sorry. Uncle Frankie had to chew me out first."

"Seriously? He chewed you out?"

"No. Not really. He just told me I should be kind to Stevie Kosgrov because he's fighting some kind of a battle I know nothing about. According to Uncle Frankie, we all are."

"Huh," says Gilda. "Never thought about it that way."

"Yeah," I say. "Me neither."

"I guess he's right."

"He usually is. That's what makes him so Uncle Frankie–ish."

"So that means you're battling something, too."

"Well, duh." I gesture at my chair.

"I meant something deeper, Jamie. Something I can't see."

"Maybe. I guess. One of the doctors up at the

Hope Trust Rehabilitation Center told me that I might have to wrestle with what they call survivor's guilt. I lived, the rest of my family died. And now, when I'm happy, I sometimes feel horrible."

"Why?"

"Because I have a chance to be happy. Mom, Dad, and Jenny lost that chance in the wreck. Forever."

"Jamie?"

"Yeah?"

"It's okay to be glad you're alive. A lot of us are very, very happy you're here. Think of all the people you make smile on a daily basis. If, like you always say, laughter is the best medicine, then you're the most incredible doctor in America, healing people all over the country. So wrestle that guilt to the ground. Maybe Stevie will let you borrow his foam rubber earmuffs and wrestling uniform."

"Just as long as I don't have to guzzle that Meathead protein shake stuff. It looks like diarrhea medicine mixed with chocolate.

"So," I say, "what's your battle, Gilda Gold?"

"You mean other than being a kid directing episodes of a hit sitcom in an adult world, having to come up with brilliant ideas for new shows, and putting up with Vincent O'Neil's bad jokes?"

"Those are just minor, everyday skirmishes," I joke. "What's your big battle? The one nobody knows about?"

She looks at me.

Thinks about saying something.

Almost does.

Turns away.

"What?" I ask.

She turns back to face me.

"This," she says.

Then she grabs the back of my head, pulls me close, and kisses me on the lips.

For a really, really, *really* long time.

Chapter 38

BREAKFAST OF COMEDIANS

Early the next morning (after smearing my lips with a ton of ChapStick), I go for breakfast at the diner, where I plan on eating crow and apologizing to Uncle Frankie.

"You were right!" I tell him. "Everybody's got something going on that nobody else knows about. Even people who probably should've known about it or seen it coming or realized how lucky they were."

Uncle Frankie takes a slow sip of coffee out of his mug.

Then he says, "Huh?"

"Never mind. It's not important. Well, it is, but hey—you have your own romantic issues to deal with."

His mug stalls in midlift again.

"Huh?"

"Gilda and me. Me and Gilda. Guess we're always the last to know. Probably because we're guys. Not Gilda. I mean you and me. We're the guys," I babble. "Anyway, like the broken elevator said to the lady on the top floor, I won't let you down, Uncle Frankie. I'm going to save Ms. Denning's library if it's the last thing I do, which I hope it isn't, because I was kind of thinking about asking Gilda to go see a movie with me this weekend. And not like that time she went with me and Gaynor and Pierce. No, sir. This time, it'll just be the two of us. Fifty-gallon drum of soda, popcorn, Junior Mints, Junior Mints *in* the popcorn—the works! But first, we need to save a library and a librarian from the barbarians in the wrestling tights and their coach. If any of those kids ever come to a class of mine again, that is. I know I wouldn't."

"Hey, Jamie?" says Uncle Frankie when I take a break to breathe. "Remember what you said when I was, you know, putting on airs to woo Ms. Denning?"

"Um, I said, 'Put on something else, because everybody can see through air'?"

Frankie shakes his head and laughs. "No, kiddo. You told me to be myself instead of some version of who I thought other people wanted me to be. Well, that's all you need to do when you teach your class. Be Jamie Grimm. You funny, remember?"

"Sometimes."

"So stop psyching yourself out. Don't try to be a professor and *tell* 'em how it's done. *Show* 'em how it's done."

"But how?" I ask. "How do I show them how?"

"When Lou Diamante, the Yo-Yo King of Queens—may he rest in peace—taught me the Breakaway Flying-Doughnut Rock-the-Kitty Cannonball, he didn't give me a lecture. He gave me a *demonstration*."

"But all the kids know my stand-up act," I say. "They've seen my routines on TV and YouTube. I have to show them something new."

"So why not compose material on the fly? Don't tell them how to come up with a joke, *show* them. Improvise like you did at the Stand Up for Books benefit last week."

"Show, don't tell," I repeat.

"Exactly. Because this is *important*. You gotta save the library, Jamie, otherwise you kids will be reading history books so old the Revolutionary War will still be a current event."

"Oh, good one-liner."

Uncle Frankie smiles. "Thanks. I was improvising."

"Well, that's what I'm going to do after school today. I'm going to take nothing and turn it into something funny."

"That's the spirit. And remember: Flora—I mean Ms. Denning—is counting on you."

"Like the busted elevator said…," I start.

"You won't let us down," Uncle Frankie finishes with a laugh.

Hey, I might've blown two classes.

But you know what they say: The third time's the charm!

Chapter 39

ROUND THREE!

I start my school day in the library.

"I'm back!" I say to Ms. Denning. "I know the last two classes weren't great, but you gotta roll with the punches. I'm pretty good at rolling, if you haven't noticed."

"You're sure, Jamie? I know you're under a lot of pressure with the TV show and—"

"Not to worry. We are going to have such an awesome class this afternoon, I guarantee the library will be packed."

"I don't know. Stevie Kosgrov scared off a lot of kids."

"He's fighting an inner battle, that's all. Stevie doesn't scare me. Although, I guess he should. At home, I've seen him crush an orange juice carton. And it was still full. But I digress."

That's when Gilda bops into the library.

She's bubblier than usual.

"Hiya, Jamie!"

"Hey!"

"I printed up flyers with 'Something Wonderful Right Away' as the headline. Sort of reminded me of the other night...on the boardwalk..."

I clear my throat. Loudly. "Ix-nay on the oardwalk-bay. There are grown-ups in the room."

"Where?" says Ms. Denning. "What are you kids cooking up now?"

"We're going to pass around these flyers today," Gilda explains. "To tell kids about today's master class with Jamie Grimm being an 'Improvisational Comedy Workshop.'"

"We'll be making up scenes, stories, and songs right on the spot," I add, "from audience suggestions. We'll be like a human makerspace, only funnier!"

"*Something Wonderful Right Away* is also the title of a book by Jeffrey Sweet," explains Gilda. "It's an oral history of improvisational comedy in

Chicago. You know, Second City and the Compass Players. They're basically the granddaddies of all comedy troupes, like the Groundlings in LA and the Upright Citizens Brigade in New York!"

"I do know," says Ms. Denning. "Ta-da! We have the book."

"No way!"

"Way. Books—they're what libraries do best."

"Ooh, can I put a hold on that one?" I ask. "Mike Nichols, Joan Rivers, Robert Klein, Tina Fey, Amy Poehler—so many funny people got their start doing improv in Chicago."

"I'll put your name at the top of the list."

"Come on, Gilda," I say. "Let's go drum up some improv students!"

During our free period, we hang up flyers.

We roll into a few classrooms (the ones where the teachers have a good sense of humor), and I do a quick bit to get kids excited about the after-school class in the library.

We hit the biology lab, where I improvise what it's like to be a cricket in a lab experiment.

"Take these pins out of my legs. All of them! I have to go be Pinocchio's conscience!"

We make sure every tray in the cafeteria is lined with a flyer—just like they do at Mickey D's with the paper place mats.

For good measure, I ask Ms. Denning to cue up a DVD of *Best in Show,* a hilarious mockumentary movie where maybe half of the hysterical dialogue was improvised on the fly.

I have a lesson plan!

I have a funny movie! (Who doesn't like funny movies?)

We are good to go.

Gilda, Gaynor, Pierce, and I slip out of our final classes a little early and are in the library at 2:38. Ms. Denning is there, too, of course.

"Thanks, you guys!" she tells us. "This is going to be amazing!"

At 2:40, the final bell rings.

We wait for the crowd to descend.

But it doesn't.

At 2:45, the only people in the library are the five of us who were there five minutes earlier. I feel all my positivity draining away like it's been flushed.

At 2:50, we're still waiting. I can't look Ms. Denning in the eye.

At 2:51, we discover why no one else, not even Vincent O'Neil, is coming to comedy class today.

The answer is outside in the parking lot.

STEVIE'S AFTER-SCHOOL SPECIAL

When we finally call it quits, turn off the lights, lock up the library, and head for the exit, we see all the kids who used to be in my comedy class lined up in the circular driveway at the front of the school.

They're all facing Stevie and Lars, who are standing beneath the flagpole. Both of them are chugging protein drinks and scrunching the plastic bottles down to the size of golf balls.

"Welcome to our new after-school class," says Lars. "Tell 'em what it's called, Stevie."

"The title of our class is How to Avoid Being Bullied After School."

"So," shouts Lars, "if you want to live to see another school day, pay attention. Lesson one. Give us all your lunch money *before* school! That way, we won't have a reason to bully you *after* school."

"Lesson two," shouts Stevie, grabbing Vincent O'Neil (who always seems to be in the front row for everything) and yanking him up onto the grass patch underneath the flagpole. "If you see something, don't say anything!"

"That's so true. Just the other day," says Vincent, who can never resist trying to crack a joke when he's in front of a crowd, "I saw Stevie and Lars punching a little old lady at the grocery store. I didn't do anything because I couldn't tell who'd started it. Thank you. I'm here all week. I think. Am I here all week, Stevie?"

"If you play by the rules," says Stevie.

"*Our* rules," adds Lars.

"Coach Ball's rules," adds Stevie.

"Yeah," says Lars. "Coach Ball is a bully's bully!"

"No problemo, guys," says Vincent as Stevie hoists him off the ground again and tosses him back into the crowd.

"Lesson number three," says Lars.

"And this is the most important lesson of them all!" says Stevie.

Lars glares at his audience. "If you don't want to be bullied after school, go home! Now!"

"And," says Stevie, "never, ever be caught dead taking some kind of stupid after-school class in the library—especially if it's being taught by that gimp Jamie Grimm. In fact, stay out of the library all the time. Libraries and books and all that other junk in there are bad for you." Stevie taps his head. "They try to make you think. School's hard enough. Why hurt your brain any more than you have to?"

Lars looks at his watch. "What's wrong with you people? Why are you still here? It's after school. Go home!"

"And pack better snacks in your lunch boxes tomorrow," says Stevie.

"Yeah," says Lars. "We're getting tired of Doritos and Ho Hos."

"If your parents are putting fruit in there instead of delicious Meathead protein shakes, you're going to be the ones to deal with our major disappointment," adds Stevie. "If you don't have a shake, we're gonna shake you down!"

"So tell your parents to buy cases of Meathead protein shakes," says Lars. "Available wherever beverages with questionable nutritional content are sold!"

They both pound their fists into their open palms.

"Go home!" shouts Lars.

Everybody flees.

"Ah, Ms. Denning."

Coach Ball just came out of the building behind us. Ms. Bumgarten is with him. Her left eye is twitching. She has her clipboard. It has a built-in calculator.

"Ms. Bumgarten and I were just walking by the library, weren't we?"

"Whatever you say, Al," says Ms. Bumgarten. Now her nose is twitching, too. I have to figure working for Coach Ball is one of those high-stress occupations. Like being a Navy SEAL.

"We both noticed that no one was using the library," says Coach Ball.

"I'd heard you had an after-school program lined

up for today," says the vice principal.

"We did," says Ms. Denning. "But, well…"

"We're really not interested in excuses, Ms. Denning," says Coach Ball. "Only results."

"Numbers don't lie or have opinions," says the vice principal, like someone brainwashed her to say it. "Numbers are unemotional." Now her nose and eye are twitching in sync.

"Ms. Bumgarten will be taking the official tally next Friday. For the school board."

"Yes, sir. I will, sir. I love numbers, sir."

"But I don't think you're going to love yours, Ms. Denning," sneers Coach Ball. "Because so far, you've done absolutely nothing to increase library usage. So far, all you've done is bring it down!"

No, that was me.

I don't want to see the look on Uncle Frankie's face when I tell him I failed.

Chapter 41

ABANDON SHIP!
THE LIBRARY, TOO!

You know what?" says Gaynor the next morning while we're walking to school.

Well, he and Pierce are walking, I'm pumping rubber. Uphill.

"What?" I say glumly.

"In, like, two weeks we're going to be back at the studio in Queens, doing the show again, right?"

"Correct," says Pierce.

"We'll have tutors on the set. They'll bring us all the books we need."

"Correct," Pierce says again.

Gaynor stops strolling, bends down, and looks

me straight in the eye. "So, Jamie, why the heck are you busting your hump to save a library you're never even going to use?"

"Good question," says Pierce, because I think he's tired of saying "correct."

"I mean, somebody on that goofy school board or whatever appointed Coach Bowling Ball to be the new principal at Long Beach Middle," says Gaynor. "If he's more interested in wrestling than learning, why should we care? *We won't be there.* We'll be at Silvercup Studios. We'll be TV stars again!"

"But what about all the kids we're leaving behind?" I say.

"Exactly," says Gaynor. "We leave 'em behind. If they want a library, why aren't they the ones fighting for it?"

"Because Uncle Frankie asked me, not them."

"And," says Pierce, "from what I have observed, your uncle's interest in the matter is fundamentally fueled by his romantic ardor for his paramour."

"Huh?" says Gaynor.

"He has the hots for Ms. Denning," says Pierce.

"Well, duh," says Gaynor. "Any fool can see that. Even me."

We reach the corner, where Gilda joins us.

"Hiya, guys," she says. "What are you three talking about?"

Gaynor looks at Pierce, who looks at me.

They both know that Gilda wants to save the library almost as much as Uncle Frankie does.

"Dumping the library," I say. "Letting Coach Ball turn it into a sweat room for no-neck Neanderthals."

Gilda laughs.

Gaynor and Pierce just look embarrassed. Then they stare at the dirt some.

"That was a joke, right?" says Gilda. "How come nobody else is laughing? You guys aren't serious, are you?"

"Um, I sort of am," says Gaynor sheepishly.

"We won't be at Long Beach Middle School this time next month," adds Pierce.

"We don't need the library," says Gaynor.

"Oh, yes, you do!" says Gilda. Then she strikes a heroic pose, dramatically pointing one finger skyward. She looks a little like the Statue of Liberty, without the green gown or torch. I swear I can hear fife and drum music in the background.

"I will now quote from an article by Stephen Segal that I read in *Philadelphia Weekly*!"

"*The* Steven Seagal?" says Gaynor. "The martial-arts dude from the action movies? Whoa!"

You wanna close my library? There's only two things stoppin' you: fear and common sense.

"I did not realize he was such a fan of libraries," adds Pierce. "Fascinating."

"Different guy," says Gilda. "Stephen with a *ph*, not a *v*."

"Oh," we all say in a disappointed way.

"According to Mr. Segal, 'a school where students are not free to use a library is not a school. It's a multiple-choice indoctrination camp.' He also says, 'The library is where students engage their own minds. The library is the place that embodies the concept of intellectual activity being something for a person to *choose*.'"

"Actually," says Pierce, "as the name implies, multiple-choice questions also allow you to choose."

"Or guess," says Gaynor. "That's what I usually do. I call them multiple-guess questions."

"You guys?" says Gilda, practically stomping her feet. "We need to save the library if it's the last thing we do!"

"Well, it might be," I joke. "Especially if Lars and Stevie have anything to do with it."

"Jamie?" she says. "We've got to do this. Before we go back to work on the show. We need to make sure the kids we leave behind have the freedom to think and read about stuff besides wrestling."

From the way she's looking at me, I can't say no.

"So let's go save a library," I say.

"How?" says Gaynor. "The after-school-class idea isn't really working."

"Then we need to try something else. Today's Friday. We have till next Friday...."

"So, let's meet up after school and brainstorm again," says Gilda. "We'll think of something. We always do."

"I'm there," I say.

"Us too," mumble Pierce and Gaynor.

"See you guys at two forty in the library," I say.

And I really meant it, too.

Too bad someone had other plans for me.

Chapter 42

ANOTHER STEPHEN

I'm in the biology lab, measuring my cricket's rear end, when the school secretary, Mrs. Kuhn, comes to the door.

"Jamie!" she says in an excited whisper. "Hollywood's calling!"

"Huh?"

"Joe Amodio! Your producer. He's in Hollywood! He wants to talk to you! On the phone! My phone! The one in the office! He's calling from Holl-leee-wooooood!" She's practically singing it.

Mr. Harris, the biology teacher, smiles and gives me a nod. "Go on, Jamie. We'll keep an eye on your cricket."

"Don't let him hop anywhere without me," I say

as I roll out the door and head down the hall behind the very excited, very giggly Mrs. Kuhn, who can't stop saying "Hollywood" every ten seconds.

Joe Amodio is the executive producer of *Jamie Funnie*. He was also the executive producer of the Planet's Funniest Kid Comic Contest. In other words, he is basically my boss.

When Joe Amodio says jump, I say, "I can't. Remember?"

"Jamie, baby!" he gushes when I pick up the school office phone and say hello. "Look out the window, what do you see?"

I look out the window. "It looks like a Hummer."

"It's a wheelchair-accessible limo, baby. For you!"

"Well, that's very nice of you, sir, but I live only a few blocks from school and—"

"It's going to take you into the city. Fifty-Fourth Street and Broadway," Mr. Amodio tells me.

"New York City? Why?"

"That's where the Ed Sullivan Theater is located. You're doing *The Late Show with Stephen Colbert* tonight. Well, actually, you're doing it this afternoon. That's when they tape."

"But I have—"

"Nothing more important to do today than promoting your TV show, am I right? Was that what you were about to say?" Mr. Amodio asks firmly.

There's a beat of ominous silence.

I swallow hard. "Yes, sir."

"That's my Jamie. Stephen's a big, big fan of your show. Can't wait to chat with you. Maybe you two can do some kind of bit together. Maybe show him how to play that wheelchair basketball game... what do you call it? Murderball! I love murderball!"

"Did you, uh, run this idea by Uncle Frankie?" I ask.

"No. Colbert doesn't want a yo-yo artist. He wants you, Jamie. Thinks you're hysterical."

The more Mr. Amodio babbles in my ear, the more I start thinking, *Hey, this might be fun.* In fact, it might be just what I need: a short break from Long Beach and libraries and Ms. Denning and Stevie and Lars and Coach Ball and crickets. It might be great to horse around onstage with the one and only Stephen Colbert. I'm a big fan of him and his show, too!

"So, when do I leave?" I ask.

"How about now?" says Mr. Amodio. "That fancy

Hummer limo out in the parking lot? They charge by the hour, Jamie baby. The meter is running!"

I probably should've let Gilda and the guys know I'd miss our after-school brainstorming session.

I probably should've told Uncle Frankie I'd miss my shift cracking jokes behind the cash register at the diner.

But, to be honest, I was so excited about doing Colbert's show, I forgot all about everybody.

Except me and Stephen Colbert!

Chapter 43

ROLLING HOME

I finish taping the show close to seven. Feeling pumped after saying good-bye to my biffle Stephen Colbert, I ask the limo driver to drop me off at the diner.

I thought it might be fun to hang out with Uncle Frankie and stay up late to watch the show together when it comes on at 11:35.

"You were funny, kid," says the limo driver. "That line about Colbert's butt? Cracked me up!"

"Thanks," I say through the partition window. "It felt good to be in front of a live studio audience again."

"By the way, would you mind autographing a couple of napkins or something back there? My kids are big fans."

"No problem, sir," I say as I scrawl my signature across a pair of napkins with the Sharpie pen I always carry. The napkins are stored right next to the snack jars and crystal goblets that I get to use to drink all the free soda I want. The snacks are free, too! Limos are genuine, first-class awesomesauce. Especially Hummer limos.

Three sodas later, we're pulling into Uncle Frankie's Good Eats by the Sea.

"Would you like me to wait for you, Mr. Grimm?"

"No, thanks. I can roll myself home from here."

It's a crisp night. The stars are twinkling. I've just guzzled free soda and gobbled free snacks in the back of a stretch military vehicle. All is right with the world.

Until I enter the diner.

"There you are!" says Uncle Frankie. "We were worried about you."

"Until we were watching the CBS news," says Gilda, "trying to see if you were in some kind of accident."

"Instead," says Pierce, "we saw a promo for your appearance on *The Late Show with Stephen Colbert.*"

"Yeah," I say. "Mr. Amodio called. Said *Jamie Funnie* needed the publicity. So I limoed into the city. Now we can all watch me and Colbert at eleven thirty-five."

"We know," says Gilda. "We saw the promo."

She doesn't look very happy. She doesn't sound very happy, either.

"Dude," says Gaynor. "You totally bailed on us. After that early-morning pep talk and everything. You bailed."

"Oh, you mean that brainstorming session we were going to do after school? We can do that tomorrow. If, you know, we're not too tired from staying up late to watch me and Stephen. We did this funny bit about—"

"Your friends pulled out all the stops," says Ms. Denning.

"Huh?"

"They got everybody to come back to the library to give you one more chance."

"One more chance at what?"

"To teach your comedy class."

"I told you guys. No more teaching. No more after-school classes."

"But we want to do that student showcase next Friday," says Gilda. "When the school board comes back. We want the library to be packed."

"Fine. We'll do the class after school on Monday. Unless, of course, Jimmy Fallon and Seth Meyers want me on their shows, too."

I smile and wait for the laugh.

There isn't one.

"That's a joke, you guys."

"No one is coming back on Monday, Jamie," says Ms. Denning. "After you didn't show today..."

Gilda sighs. "We promised everybody that the best comic in your after-school class would get a walk-on part on your TV show."

"But then," says Pierce, "there wasn't any class."

"Everybody thinks you're totally bogus, dude," adds Gaynor.

"You had a shot, Jamie," says Uncle Frankie. "One last chance to save the library. And you blew it."

"It's not my fault," I say, sounding defensive, because, well, I am. "I didn't even know about the class!"

When people attack, that's what you do. You get defensive.

"Because you left," Gilda says stubbornly.

"I did what my boss, Joe Amodio, told me to do," I tell them. "I went on the Stephen Colbert show to promote *my* TV show, the one that pays all our salaries and makes this diner famous for something besides yo-yos and greasy spoons!"

Yes, sometimes when you get defensive, you can also get hurtful.

"You did what your boss told you to do?" says Gilda semisarcastically and seriously disappointed. "What about what your heart told you to do?"

"All my heart said was *lub-dub, lub-dub, lub-dub*. And then it said it a little faster when I was on the set with Stephen, because I was pumped to be performing in front of a national TV audience instead of pretending to be a teacher, which is something I'm not and never will be. Ever since that wreck on the highway, I'm nothing but a crippled kid cracking corny jokes in a wheelchair, and that's all I'll ever be."

"That's not what I see," says Gilda softly.

"Then you need to open your eyes!"

I whip around fast because I don't want everybody to see me crying. I give both tires a good double pump, fly out the door, and head for the boardwalk.

This time, I hope Cool Girl isn't there.

I also hope Gilda doesn't come chasing after me.

This time, I just want to be alone.

Chapter 4

NOT-SO-CRAZY BOB

To be super certain no one will join me on the boardwalk, I find a totally random bench.

One I've never been to before.

One without even a streetlamp nearby.

The only light is coming from the moon, and it's doing its best to hide behind clouds because it knows I want to be alone.

Because that's how I feel. Alone.

No one knows what I'm going through. What I've *been* through.

Okay, maybe Uncle Frankie does.

And Gilda.

And the Smileys.

And Gaynor and Pierce. Maybe even Vincent O'Neil.

Maybe I'm lucky to have friends who care about me so much. Maybe I'm just too embarrassed to admit I let everybody down. That by going into New York City to do the Stephen Colbert show, I might've cost Uncle Frankie a second chance at love.

"Hiya, comedian kid."

I look up. It's Crazy Bob.

Only he doesn't look so crazy anymore.

"I'm glad I found you," says Bob. "I've been looking all over for you."

"Really?"

"Oh, yeah. Do you know that you and your goofy friend—the girl with the frizzy hair and the baseball cap—you two are the only kids who ever tossed coins into my cup?"

"No. I did not know that."

"So, do you know where Miss Frizzy is tonight?"

"Yes," I say. "Somewhere very disappointed in me."

Bob nods. "That'll happen. Anyway, can you pass on a message?"

"I guess."

"Good, good. Okay, here's the deal. I'm leaving the boardwalk. I just wanted to thank you two for being decent human beings."

"Um, you're welcome, I guess. Where are you headed?"

Bob shrugs. "To whatever's at the other end of this boardwalk. You see, a while back, I was in a spaceship, which, by the way, looked nothing like a flying saucer. More like a meteor. *Zooooom*. You know? With a fiery tail?"

O-kay. Maybe Bob still is a little crazy.

"Me and my fellow aliens were flying from

Galaxatron to Cyrus Major 14," he continues. "That's a star cluster in the Noonoonobby Quadrant."

"Riiight."

"There was an accident. We were flying too low and collided with something. Could've been a flock of seagulls. Anyway, the spaceship crash-landed out there in the ocean. Everybody else on board? Well, let's just say they weren't as lucky as me."

"You were the sole survivor?"

He nods. "That's why I've spent my days here on the boardwalk, telling people that the Galaxatronians were coming back, because I wanted to see my friends again. My family. But today, I realized something: They're not coming back. They can't. But you know what?"

"What?"

"I don't have to stay here. I can move on. I think it's what they'd like me to do."

"Yeah," I say, smiling for the first time in about an hour. "I think you're right. It's okay to be glad you're alive. That's what my friend Gilda told me, too."

"She the one with the frizzy hair?"

"Yeah."

"She's a keeper, kid."

"I know."

Bob stands up from the bench. Reaches into his pocket.

"Here you go, kid."

He hands me a grubby quarter. Probably one of the ones I gave him. "Buy your girlfriend something nice. Maybe one of those jawbreaker-sized gum balls."

"Thanks," I say. "I think I will."

Bob gives me a quick salute and drifts down the boardwalk.

Is he really an alien whose spaceship crashed into the Atlantic Ocean? I doubt it. But I figure that's the story he made up to help him deal with whatever horrible loss *he'd* gone through, which sounded pretty close to mine. It's like Uncle Frankie says: Always be kind, because everyone you meet is fighting a hard battle you know nothing about.

Even Not-So-Crazy Bob.

I pull out my phone and call Gilda.

"Hi," she says when she answers.

"Hi. I think I owe you a giant gum ball."

Chapter 45

QUITTING TIME?

Gilda and I talk and text all night.

Neither one of us watches me on *The Late Show with Stephen Colbert.*

"I'm sorry," I tell her.

"Yep," she says. "Sometimes you totally are."

Then we laugh.

Then we move on.

Gilda has, once again, totally forgiven me.

And yes, me being me, she has to do that a lot!

We return to school on Monday with a *renewed* renewed sense of purpose and urgency. We will save the library. We will stop Ms. Denning from leaving town. We will buy a humongous gum ball with Not-So-Crazy Bob's gnarly quarter—but only after we do all the other stuff.

We have five days.

You can do a lot in five days. Heck, I've even received spam e-mails telling me I can lose all the weight I want in five days—not that I'm really interested in doing that, but it is good to know that I could if I ever wanted to.

During our free period, we head to the library to do the brainstorming we planned to do last Friday. I vaguely remember that we originally met here to brainstorm ideas for *Jamie Funnie,* but that would have to wait.

The library—and Uncle Frankie—needed me more.

"Maybe the whole after-school-classes idea *was* the wrong angle," says Gilda as we make our way down the hall. "We need to save the library as a library."

"But you're right," I tell her. "The stand-up comedy showcase is still our best chance for getting a ton of kids in here on the big day."

We roll into the library.

And see a bunch of construction guys stretching measuring tapes against the walls and bookcases.

Ms. Denning is at her desk, packing her tape dispenser and Chinese waving-kitty clock into a cardboard box.

"Ms. Denning?" says Gilda. "What's going on?"

"I'm following Jamie's lead," she says. "I'm giving up."

"Um, over the weekend I totally changed my mind," I say. "I'm not doing that giving-up thing anymore. We're going to save this library!"

"Thanks, you guys," says Ms. Denning with a sigh. "But I think it'll be too little, too late. If Coach Ball is so dead set against a library, I'm not sure I want to be a librarian at his school anymore."

"It's not *his* school," says Gilda. "It's ours!"

"No, Gilda. Right now, Coach Ball is the one who gets to call all the shots."

"But what about Uncle Frankie?" I ask.

"I'll miss him. I'll miss you guys. I'll even miss Vincent O'Neil. But I'm tired of fighting a losing battle."

"So," I say, "let's turn it into a winning battle."

She shakes her head. "Impossible."

"Impossible? Oh, you mean like me winning a national comedy contest or Gilda winning a full-ride scholarship to UCLA. But guess what? Both of those impossible things turned out to be possible."

"Impossible is just an opinion," says Gilda.

Ms. Denning smiles weakly. "I used to believe the same thing."

That's when Coach Ball strides into the library.

"Ms. Denning?" he barks. "Have you called Goodwill or the Salvation Army? Come next Monday, we need somebody to haul away all these books!"

"It's on my to-do list," she says, glancing back at us.

That's when Gilda and I realize: We need a to-do list of our own!

Chapter 46

SECRET ANNOUNCEMENT

Item number one on our list: Make a major announcement.

And we need to do it undetected by Coach Ball or his poor sidekick, Ms. Bumgarten.

"The vice principal is in the nurse's office," says Gilda. "Apparently, working for a boss who's also a bully will give you stomach issues."

"Speaking of the big bully, where's Coach Ball?" I ask.

"He's locked inside his office with a pair of muscleheads whose arms look like they're made out of bowling balls," reports Gaynor. He's been tracking the principal for us. "Whoever the two jocks are, they came to school in one of those vans with a humongous ad for Meathead protein shakes."

"That means they might be in there for a while," says Pierce. "Coach Ball seems quite dedicated to that particular beverage."

"Even though it tastes like glue soup," I add.

"You've tried it?" asks Gilda, surprised.

"Once. Stevie has a case of the stuff crammed into the Smileys' refrigerator. Hoped it might, you know, give me muscles where I need them most." I nod toward my legs. "So I gagged down a sip. Thought I was going to die. I can't believe it's all Stevie drinks or eats every day."

"Well," says Gilda, "if Coach Ball is busy, *we* need to get busy!"

Fortunately, it's lunchtime. Half the school is in the cafeteria. And anything we tell them, they'll tell to the other half, who eat lunch later.

I autograph an eight-by-ten glossy for Gus the janitor. (His daughter is a big fan of *Jamie Funnie*). He brings me the cordless microphone they use for assemblies.

"You're not going to make another puddle, are you, kid?" he asks before turning it over.

"No, sir. Just a major announcement."

"And Coach Ball says it's okay?"

I can't lie. "Not really."

Gus shrugs. "Works for me. I'll be honest with you here, Jamie. I don't really like our new principal. He pinned me to the floor the other day. And it was a bathroom floor that needed mopping, if you catch my drift."

I nod so he'll spare me the gory details.

Gus hands me the mic.

"Knock 'em dead, kiddo!"

I roll to the center of the room.

"Hey, everybody. Don't want to disturb your lunch. I know it's beanie-weenie day. Personal fave of mine. Anyway, I just wanted to let you know, we are going to host a comedy showcase in the library this coming Friday."

Silence.

After my terrible comedy classes, I can't blame them for doubting me. I even doubted myself.

Gilda grabs the microphone from me. "One of our lucky participants will be chosen, at random, to make a special walk-on appearance on the hit TV show *Jamie Funnie*!"

"Wow," I say when Gilda hands me back the mic. "A walk-on? I wish I could play that part!"

Everybody laughs.

"Good one, Jamie," shouts Vincent O'Neil, who, of course, is sitting in the front row again. The guy *always* gets the best seat in the house.

"And this time," I say, "I'm not teaching any comedy classes."

"Woo-hoo!" shouts Vincent.

"Nope. You guys are going to school *me!* I want to hear jokes about stuff that's never been joked about before. I want you to surprise me with fresh, new material about subjects that you wouldn't think would be funny. Everything from archaeology to zoology and all the -ologies in between."

"Why?" asks Vincent.

"I guess I'm just tired of the same old knock-knock jokes and puns. And I want you guys to learn to find the funny in everything. It might not be easy, but it's worth trying."

"Wait a second," says Max Garner, a kid in the seventh grade. "How are we supposed to make jokes about junk we don't know anything about?"

"Easy," I say. "The library. Do a little research. Remember, jokes start with a fact or observation. Then all you have to do is give it a little twist or a funny spin. And don't forget—everything you've ever wanted to know is in that room."

"All of it?" says Max Garner skeptically.

"Okay. Technically, not everything, because like they say, people learn something new every day. But we've got enough information in there to launch a bazillion jokes! So let's get to work!"

Gilda grabs the microphone again. "You heard Jamie! Let's do it, people!" she shouts. "Show me the funny! Win a spot on a national TV show!"

Whole tables abandon their beanie weenies and dash up the hall to the library.

If this TV-director thing doesn't work out, I really think Gilda would be a better coach than Coach Ball.

Not that it would be very hard.

Chapter 47

NERDY JOKE-ATHON

For the next few days, the library is packed.

Everybody is in there grabbing books and trying to work up jokes about subjects no professional comedian has ever joked about before. For instance, atoms. Seriously. When was the last time you heard a guy on TV joking about protons, neutrons, and electrons? But right after Vincent O'Neil grabs a book in the science section, he comes at me with a joke that's not half bad.

"So, Jamie, listen to this—two atoms are walking along. One of them says, 'Oh, no, I think I lost an electron.' 'Are you sure?' says the other. 'Yes, I'm positive.'"

If you haven't gotten to that part in science class

yet, atoms change their charge from negative to positive when they lose an electron. Look, you're learning something—consider this the world's funniest textbook!

"I've been checking out the history of ancient Rome," says Max Garner.

"What've you got?" I ask him.

"How was the Roman Empire cut in half?"

"I don't know. How?"

"With a pair of Caesars!"

Okay. It's kind of corny. But everybody's having fun learning new stuff and giving it a goofy gag line.

"Jamie, this is amazing," says Ms. Denning, who's overwhelmed by the number of students swarming through her stacks.

"We just rebranded the library," says Gilda. "Instead of an information resource center, it's a joke creation lab!"

"Well," says Ms. Denning, "I've always said learning should be fun. You guys are making it funny, too!"

I roll around the room. Check in with everybody doing research.

"This is great, you guys," I tell them all.

"Remember, the comedy showcase is Friday, so don't tell me *all* your jokes. Save some for the show."

And then I'm hit with the biggest surprise of all.

Stevie Kosgrov bursts into the library and stomps straight toward me.

Uh-oh.

He must've been sent by Coach Ball to shut down our library joke lab. Looks like my teaching—and breathing—days are officially over.

I close my eyes, not wanting to see the Meathead-protein-shake-powered fist coming at me.

"I need to hide!" he whispers.

I open my eyes. "Whaaat?"

He looks around quickly like a nervous meerkat. "From Coach Ball. This is the last place on earth he'd look for me."

I smile because Stevie is reminding me of when *I* had to hide in the library from *him*.

"So, uh, why do you need to hide from your coach?" I ask.

"He's such a big bully. And I didn't meet my sales quota this week. You should've seen what he did to Lars Johannsen!"

"Really? What are you guys selling?"

"Meathead protein shakes. I hate those things. They're like Milk of Magnesia but without the minty aftertaste."

When he says that, a couple of kids close by chuckle.

"It's hard to describe how bad it tastes," Stevie babbles on. "But have you ever sucked on any of your dirty socks when they were wet?"

Everybody who can hear starts cracking up.

Well, what do you know? Stevie funny.

"The other day," Stevie continues, "I said to Coach Ball, 'I want to know what's in those shakes.' And he said, 'No, you don't.' When the chemistry teacher asked us, 'What explosive result do you get when you mix sodium and water?' I told him, 'Meathead protein shakes!' When Coach Ball asked me why I didn't want to be on the wrestling team anymore, I told him I didn't have the time or the crayons to explain it to him."

The kids in the library are busting their guts laughing.

"Killer material, Stevie," says Vincent O'Neil. "You funny!"

"Really?" says Stevie with a smile, which is something the Smiley family seldom does. Then he turns to me.

"I want to do like you do, Jamie," he says. "You crack jokes about whatever's bothering you or whoever's trying to knock you on your butt. Heck, you even make fun of me."

He leans in and grabs me by the shirt with both hands.

Only this time I can tell: Stevie Kosgrov doesn't want to heave me out of my chair and toss me sideways like a lumpy sack of potatoes.

"Help me, cuz! I need to crack jokes before I crack up!" he pleads.

Is this real life? Stevie Kosgrov is begging for my help!

I think back to all the terrible things Stevie's done to me and other kids. Nobody would blame me for turning him down.

But I remember what Uncle Frankie said. Everyone has their battles, and everyone deserves a chance.

So I say the words I might regret for the rest of my life....

"No problem, Stevie," I tell him. "Welcome to the School of Laughs!"

Chapter 48

STEVIE FUNNIE!

Thursday after school, we organize a dress rehearsal for the big comedy showcase on Friday—the day Mrs. Critchett and the rest of the school board will be coming back to see how many students are actually using the library.

How many kids show up to the dress rehearsal?

Just about all of them! Everybody, including Stevie Kosgrov, is having so much fun making jokes about what random but cool stuff they've learned. I think the only student not in the library is Lars Johannsen. Then again, he called in sick.

"A very bad case of stomach cramps and gas," says Stevie. "Totally powered by Meathead protein shakes."

According to Stevie, those shakes will definitely make you "go, go, go." As in, to the bathroom. Constantly!

"Lars drinks, like, fifteen bottles a day," Stevie tells me. "That's why his breath stinks so bad."

"It does?" I ask.

"Big-time," says Stevie. "His breath is so bad, I never know whether to give him Tic Tacs or toilet paper."

I laugh. "You're definitely funny, Stevie."

"Thanks."

"And you'll see—popping punch lines is more fun than punching people."

"I wish Lars could be here," says Stevie. "He could use funny lessons, too. It's not easy being bullied by somebody bigger and meaner than you."

Right. Tell me about it.

"Well," I suggest, "maybe when Lars is feeling better, you can tutor him."

"Yeah. 'Each one teach one' is a better motto than 'Each one beat one.'"

By the end of the day, Stevie Kosgrov is my star student. Maybe it's something about his size. Or how tiny the microphone looks in his hand. Or his warped view of the world. Whatever it is, during the final run-through, Stevie Kosgrov kills, big-time. And, in a first for him, he does it without actually injuring anybody.

"You know," he tells the packed library, "when you drink all those Meathead protein shakes all day, every day, your breath smells so bad, you could win the Hunger Games just by yawning."

Everybody's laughing instead of trembling with fear—a first for Long Beach Middle School's longest-reigning bully.

When Coach Ball was our age, he was such a jock. Do you know what he got on his SATs? Drool!

It's sort of fun to see Stevie work out all his bottled-up hostility against Coach Ball. In the School of Laughs, he's just cracking jokes—not somebody's ribs.

"The other day," he tells his audience, "Coach Ball said, 'Stevie, I'm not supposed to let you wrestle anymore, since you failed math. But I need you on the team. So, what I have to do is ask you a math question, and if you get it right, you can stay on the team.' I said, 'Okay, Coach.' He looked me in the eye and said, 'Okay, concentrate really, really hard: What is two plus two?' I thought for a second and answered, 'Four!' Coach looked stunned. 'Did you say "four"?' He said it like he couldn't believe it. That's when Lars started screaming, 'Come on, Coach. Give him another chance!'"

Everybody laughs.

Me? I'm grinning from ear to ear. I'm glad I gave my cousin Stevie another chance. I'm also glad he let me live long enough to give it to him.

"All right, everybody," I say at the end of the run-through. "Tomorrow's the big day. We'll do the show for the school board during seventh period, and then Gilda will draw a name out of her hat to see which one of you will be a guest star on *Jamie Funnie* when we start shooting new shows."

"Is she going to pull it out of her Boston Red Sox hat?" asks Stevie.

"Yep," says Gilda, probably remembering the time not so long ago when Stevie threatened her with serious bodily harm for supporting a Boston team anywhere within one hundred miles of Yankee Stadium. "You got a problem with that, Stevie?"

"Nope. But it reminds me of a joke I just made up over in the geography section. How do you know if somebody's from Boston?"

"How?" I ask.

"They think Philadelphia is the Midwest."

I smile. Not just because Stevie's joke is semifunny.

Nope. I'm feeling super confident: Tomorrow, when those school board members show up and Ms. Bumgarten makes her official tally of all these kids in this packed room, we're going to be okay because we're using the library to save the library!

Chapter 49

ALL THE RAGE

The next morning, Stevie actually walks to school with me and my friends.

"This isn't some kind of stealthy, undercover bully tactic, is it?" asks Gaynor. "You're seriously not going to beat us up?"

"Nah," says Stevie. "My bullying days are behind me, guys. I'm going to become a comedian like Lewis Black. He's always so angry. He even did the voice for the red guy, Anger, in that Pixar movie *Inside Out*. I could do that. I could yell at a camera better than anyone."

"So you're not going to shake us down if we refuse to drink those vile Meathead protein shakes?" asks Pierce.

Congratulations, middle school cafeterias of America. You've officially ruined pizza and nachos! How is that even possible?

"Nope. But Coach Ball might," says Stevie. "He really likes those muscleheads from the Meathead company. I think they like him, too. They even bought him a new car."

"No way!" says Gilda.

"Way," says Stevie. "Or, since we're talking about protein shakes, *whey!*"

"Um, Stevie?" I say.

"Yeah?"

"Jokes that rely on spelling don't really work when you say them out loud."

Stevie nods and pulls out a little spiral notebook to jot that down. "Duly noted, Coach. Thanks for the tip."

Who *is* this guy?

Stevie continues. "Now Coach Ball drives a Maserati convertible that's even cooler than the cherry-red Mustang in Jamie's bedroom."

"You mean the garage," I say.

Stevie shrugs. "You could've bunked in my room."

I grin. "No, thanks. I like my roommate. Mustangs don't punch."

When we get to school, I check out Coach Ball's

new Maserati in the parking lot. It is a sweet ride—
even with the Meathead decals on the doors.

I roll into the library.

Ms. Denning and Uncle Frankie finish hanging
up a banner that says DEWEY LIKE TO LAUGH? I guess
because of the library's Dewey decimal system.
Or maybe Scrooge McDuck's grandnephews, Huey,
Louie, and Dewey.

"Mrs. Kressin, the drama club teacher, let me
borrow her sound system," says Ms. Denning,
pushing a cart with an amplifier and speaker.

"Where do you want this?" asks Uncle Frankie,
pushing another cart with an LED projector on it.

"Park it over there, Francis," says Ms. Denning. "We'll turn it on later and use it as a spotlight for the kids."

"I love it," I say. "Now you guys are improvising, too!"

"So when's the big show, Flora?" asks Uncle Frankie.

"Seventh period. The last period of the day. Most of the teachers are giving their students passes so they can come down here and take part in the comedy showcase."

"They're helping you out?" says Uncle Frankie. "Aren't they afraid of what their boss, Coach Ball, might do if he finds out?"

"Maybe," says Ms. Denning. "But they're more afraid of what will happen to everybody's education at Long Beach Middle if he gets his way and we lose our library. Who knows what part of the school he'll get rid of next!"

Chapter 50

SHOWTIME!

At lunch, kids all over the cafeteria are trying out their showcase material one last time.

Some jokes are so funny, whole tables are rolling on the floor with laughter, which is usually my job. Well, the rolling-on-the-floor part, anyway.

Everyone's having such a good time that they don't even notice how terrible the food is. I'm glad I asked them to write jokes about nonobvious things. Making fun of the cafeteria lunches would be so easy, I'd have to mark it as cheating.

At sixth period, kids start filing into the library.

"Everybody work on your material or grab a book to come up with a new joke," I suggest. "We've got forty-two minutes until showtime!"

When the class change bell rings, it really looks like the whole entire student body is streaming into the library. The place is packed. There is no way the school board will ever vote to shut it down!

"You done good, Jamie," Uncle Frankie tells me. He never misses any of my performances. "Real good!"

The class bell rings at 2:15. It's go time!

But Mrs. Critchett and the school board aren't here.

At 2:20, they still haven't shown up.

"Maybe they're running a little late," I tell the crowd. "Maybe they saw a fire truck and all went racing home to make sure their house wasn't the one on fire."

My lame joke gets a few chuckles. The nervous kind.

"Maybe we should make a few phone calls," Uncle Frankie suggests to Ms. Denning.

"Not yet, Francis," she tells him. "Let's give them a few more minutes."

Finally, at 2:30, Ms. Bumgarten marches into the library. The crowd parts. She comes up to me, motions for the microphone. I hand it to her.

"Congratulations, Ms. Denning," she says. "You've certainly turned things around in here."

Everybody applauds. Uncle Frankie tosses in a couple of "woo-hoos!"

"Thank you, Janeece," says Ms. Denning. "The kids are eager to learn, and there's no better place than a library to learn whatever you want to know."

"I commend your efforts."

"We're going to put on a comedy show for the school board!" shouts Vincent O'Neil. "Only they won't be *bored* when they hear our jokes!"

Ms. Bumgarten shakes her head. "Sorry, children. There will be no comedy show today. The school board has been called into an emergency session. They will not be able to visit the library, and have therefore, at Coach Ball's suggestion, decided to use my earlier library usage statistics to help them reach their decision. Kindly disperse. You are dismissed for the day."

There's a stunned silence. I can't believe everything has gone so wrong so quickly.

Feeling a deep sense of dread, I ask, "Um, when exactly did you take attendance?"

"While you and your friends were off filming your TV show," she says. "When *nobody* was using the library."

Chapter 51

EMERGENCY ACTION

Emergency session?" hollers Stevie, balling up his fists as his face turns redder than a ketchup stain on Santa's suit. "I'll give them an emergency!"

I touch his elbow. "Don't give in to the dark side of the Force, Stevie," I say in my best Jedi Knight voice. "Make jokes, not fists."

He relaxes. A little.

"What the heck is goin' on here, ma'am?" demands Uncle Frankie. "What emergency could possibly be more important than all these kids trying to save their school's library? Is somebody having a heart attack or something?"

"No," says the vice principal. "However, Coach Ball has an emergency with regard to Long Island interscholastic athletics. Apparently, the wrestling season starts next week. Therefore, he demanded that the school board meet immediately and vote to give him the sweat room he needs to, and I quote, 'bring home the championship trophy.'"

"He's also going to need some new wrestlers!" shouts Stevie. "Because I quit!"

"I'm sorry to hear that, Stephen," says Ms. Bumgarten. "I was hoping that wrestling might cure some of your disciplinary issues."

"It doesn't have to!" says Stevie. "Comedy already has!"

"But we were told that today was the big day," says Gilda. "We've been building to this showcase for weeks. Surely, the board can't make a decision this important without all the facts."

"But they have the facts," says the vice principal. "As I told you, I gave them my earlier numbers."

"You gave them old news," says Uncle Frankie.

"I'm sorry. I wish I could give them today's updated statistics, but Coach Ball forced my hand. He said there was a time crunch. And to prove his point, he crushed my desk clock. He is quite difficult to work for. I eat two dozen Rolaids every day. My hair is falling out in clumps...."

"So he's bullying you, too?" says Ms. Denning.

"Yes," says Ms. Bumgarten. "Horribly."

"Where's the board meeting?" I ask.

"In the cafeteria. Coach Ball is serving refreshments. Corn dogs and Meathead protein shakes."

Stevie urps and almost hurls.

"They will be considering a motion to eliminate the library line item from the school budget in order that Coach Ball might use that money, plus a generous endowment from an outside sponsor, to construct the Meathead Wrestling Room."

"When's the vote?" I ask.

Ms. Bumgarten checks her watch. "In ten minutes. No, nine."

Nine minutes?

I've got to think of a plan B, fast. Because plan A just went out the window, even though the library doesn't have any windows, which is why Coach Ball wants to turn it into his sweatshop!

"Again, I'm sorry," says Ms. Bumgarten. "I think what you kids have done here at the library is incredible. I wish it didn't have to end this way."

And then she leaves—sucking all the joy, laughter, and energy out of the room.

Gilda spins on her heel, grabs both my armrests, and leans in. "Jamie? You've got to do something!"

"Everybody follow me!" I shout. "I have a new idea. We're taking this show on the road!"

"Vegas?" asks Vincent O'Neil eagerly.

"Nope! The cafeteria. We're not quitting. If the school board won't come to us, we'll go to the school board! Quitters never win, and winners never quit. Right, Ms. Denning?"

She looks at me. Her eyes are kind of watery. Uncle Frankie's, too.

"You're wonderful, Jamie Grimm!" she says, sounding choked up. "Come on, Francis. Help me pack up."

"Your desk?" says Uncle Frankie.

"No, that banner! We need it for when we march into the cafeteria!"

Gilda grabs my armrests again, to give me a quick pep talk, I'm guessing.

I would be wrong.

She leans in to kiss me.

In public. In front of the entire student body, Uncle Frankie, *and* Ms. Denning.

Now I'm the one with a face redder than Santa's ketchup-stained suit.

Chapter 52

ROAD SHOW

Uncle Frankie and Ms. Denning take down the DEWEY LIKE TO LAUGH? banner and stretch it out between them to lead the parade.

Gaynor grabs the rolling sound equipment cart. Vincent packs up our spotlight—the portable LED projector.

I roll over to the magazine rack.

"What are you doing?" asks Gilda.

"Some quick research," I tell her as I flip through the pages of a business magazine that just caught my eye. There's a big logo for Meathead protein shakes on the cover.

"Research? Now? Why?"

"Because I need some new knowledge for my part of the show."

"Um, couldn't you have done that a long time ago?"

"Nope." I furiously flip through the glossy pages. "I just got the idea for this bit from Stevie, like, two minutes ago! Jimmy?" I call to Pierce. "I need some more information. Fast."

"Then I'm your man." Pierce links his hands together to crack his knuckles.

I give him keywords to search.

"On it!" He bustles off to the library's computers.

"Bring me everything you can in five minutes!"

"No problem," says Pierce. "I'll out-Google Google!"

I roll up the magazine. Jam it into the backpack strapped behind my chair.

"You guys," Vincent O'Neil says to the crowd of would-be comics, "the cafeteria will be the perfect place for our show! It'll be just like doing dinner theater! We can crack food jokes, too!"

"No," I say. "Stick to the smart stuff you learned in the library."

"And be sure to cite your sources!" adds Ms. Denning. (What can I say? She's a librarian. They're all about the source citing.)

Uncle Frankie and Ms. Denning lead the way, carrying that DEWEY banner. I roll right behind them. Our five-hundred-plus library-loving comedians march down the halls behind me. If we had a few balloons and a brass band, we could be the Macy's Thanksgiving Day Parade!

When we enter the cafeteria, we can see Coach Ball and his two musclehead friends in flashy jackets with Meathead logos on them. They're addressing Mrs. Lexi Critchett and the rest of the school board, who are seated at two tables. And, yes, they all have corn dogs. Tater Tots, too. Ms. Bumgarten is standing behind one of the tables, consulting her watch and making notes on a clipboard.

"Ms. Denning?" snarls Coach Ball as our parade fans out to fill the cafeteria. "What's the meaning of this?"

"Hit me, Gus!" I say, rolling to the center of the room.

"You got it, Jamie!"

The janitor tosses me that cordless mic again. I'm on.

"A very good question, Principal Ball," I say.

Gaynor thumps on the projector—our improvised spotlight. I roll into the circle of bright-white illumination. I can tell the school board members are confused, so I jump right in.

"However," I say, "if you're really searching for the meaning of this—not to mention the *truth* of

271

this—you should be in the library, not the cafeteria. That place has dictionaries full of meanings and books full of truths. That's why all of us were in the library today, doing research. Isn't that right, Ms. Bumgarten?"

"Yes. All five hundred and thirty-two of you."

Coach Ball whirls around to stare at his vice principal. He seems stunned by that statistic.

"I did a quick head count," says Ms. Bumgarten, brandishing a shiny silver hand clicker. She glances at the digital readout. "Sorry. Five hundred and thirty-three. I forgot to count myself. I found a very interesting recipe for banana cream pie in the cookbook section."

"You see, ladies and gentlemen," I tell the board, "this school *needs* a library. It's the one place we can explore whatever we want to explore, learn whatever we want to learn—even if some people don't want us learning it."

"It's a great place for making up jokes, too," adds Vincent O'Neil.

"That's right," I say. "How can you make up new material if you don't discover new information? Like this article right here."

I show everybody that business magazine I found.

"Jamie?" hollers Pierce, running into the cafeteria. "I found a ton more."

"Can you cite your sources?" I ask.

"Yep!"

"Good work, Mr. Pierce," says Ms. Denning.

Pierce hands me a stack of printouts, a newspaper ad, and a couple of magazines.

I scan them all as fast as I can.

"Mr. Grimm?" says Mrs. Critchett. "You know I'm a big fan of your show—"

"Me too," says another board member, shooting me a thumbs-up. "You funny!"

"But," says Mrs. Critchett, "we have some urgent business to attend to this afternoon. The wrestling season is about to start and—"

"I know!" I tell her. "But this is urgent, too! Maybe more important than anything else on your agenda."

There's no time for me to write up a new bit from all the library material Pierce and I found.

I'm going to have to improvise.

Again!

Chapter 53

DID YOU HEAR THE ONE ABOUT THE COACH WHO MIGHT BE A CROOK?

Any of you folks read *Biz Wiz Weekly*?" I ask my crowd.

"That's a magazine for children," says a member of the school board.

"I know. Must be why it's in our library. Lots of children in this school, every day. Lots in the library, too. Especially now that Ms. Denning has turned it into a real information commons, with collaboration stations, a makerspace, and lots of good books and informative magazines."

I hold up the *Biz Wiz Weekly* magazine with the Meathead logo on the cover. "Now, even though this is a business magazine, there's some pretty funny stuff in here. In fact, some of it's hysterical. Especially this article about Meathead protein shakes."

Behind me, I hear Stevie urp again. It's an instant gag reflex whenever anybody even mentions the shakes he's been chugging.

"I thought youse burned all them magazines," one of Coach Ball's muscleheads says to the other.

"I thought youse was going to do that!" says the other. He turns to Coach Ball. "Al? What's that magazine doing in your library?"

"I don't know," says Coach Ball. "I never go into the library...."

"But *we* all do," I say. I open the magazine to the article.

"That article is full of lies!" shouts one of the muscleheads.

"You mean this bit here," I say, "where it talks about how you guys bombed in the college and high school markets, so you decided to go after—and I quote—'dumb middle school kids who will do whatever their even dumber coaches and school-yard bullies tell them to do'?"

Coach Ball stands up, glares at the muscleheads. "You two saying I'm dumber than these numskull kids?"

"So, Jamie?" says Stevie, stepping up to join me in the spotlight.

"Yeah, Stevie?"

Suddenly we're a comedy team like Abbott and Costello, Frick and Frack, Cheech and Chong, Key and Peele.

"How does Meathead get a dumb coach to tell us dumb kids to drink the dumb stuff?" asks Stevie.

"They pay him," I say.

"Money?"

I smile widely at the crowd. "Nope. They give him a Maserati."

"Is that a type of pasta?" says Stevie, playing

dumb. (Or maybe he isn't playing. Hard to tell with my cousin.)

"No. A Maserati is an Italian sports car, Stevie. In this case, a red convertible."

"Wait a second," says Stevie, looking surprised. "I saw one of those out in the parking lot. Somebody parked it in Coach Ball's space."

"Yep. That would be Coach Ball."

Stevie hams up his part by putting his hands on his cheeks. "No way! It looked too expensive for a coach's car."

"You're right," I say, digging out the newspaper clipping Pierce handed me. "Looks like Coach Ball's Maserati GranTurismo convertible out there in the parking lot has a list price of between one hundred forty-five thousand and one hundred eighty thousand dollars."

Stevie whistles.

"I can explain!" says Coach Ball. "That car was a gift. From, uh, my mother."

"Really?" I say. "Is she the one who asked you to put the Meathead decals on the doors?"

Stevie takes over. "And is your mother the one who told you to make me and Lars beat up any kids who weren't buying Meathead shakes on a regular basis? Because that doesn't sound too motherly to me."

"Hey, Stevie?" I say.

"Yeah, Jamie?"

"Know what Coach Ball's motto is?"

"If at first you don't succeed, lie, lie again!"

Stevie and I take a bow while our classmates applaud and the school board stares at us in shock.

That's a wrap!

Chapter 5

HYSTERIA IN THE CAFETERIA

So this is when Coach Ball goes a little nutsy.

His eyes turn into bulging, bloodshot Ping-Pong balls.

I think he's been chugging those Meathead protein shakes right along with Stevie and Lars. I also think there might be some kind of chemical in them that short-circuits your brain and makes you kind of cray-cray. The same kind of stuff that turns mild-mannered physicist Bruce Banner into the Incredible Hulk, or Dr. Jekyll into Mr. Hyde.

Whatever it is, Coach Ball goes from annoyed middle school principal to enraged maniac monster in under five seconds.

"Kosgrov, you big, fat dummy!" he screams. "You

let the team down! You broke your sacred athlete's oath by ratting me out and telling these wimpy eggheads about my Maserati! Your big, fat mouth needs to be shut before you destroy me and my mighty wrestling-team dreams!"

He leaps across the room and pounces on Stevie.

But Stevie, who's been off the shakes for about a week, isn't as shaky as he used to be. In fact, he's pretty nimble.

He jukes sideways, catches one of Coach Ball's arms, and flips him onto his back.

Coach Ball tumbles into a roll, springs back to his feet, spins around, and charges at Stevie, locking him in a bear hug. The two of them dance around the floor, legs tangling, each one trying to trip up the other.

Uncle Frankie charges up to pull Coach Ball off Stevie, but the wrestling pair bumps into him and knocks him down to the floor. Ms. Denning runs to make sure he's all right and to stop him from trying again. His bad heart means that he can't exert himself too much.

The school board members are gasping in horror.

I've never felt so helpless or useless in my life. I'm stuck in my wheelchair. There is absolutely nothing I can do to help Stevie outwrestle his wrestling coach.

I'm pretty sure fighting with a student immediately after basically admitting that you took bribes from shady protein shake dealers is considered conduct unbecoming to a middle school principal, maybe even grounds for dismissal. But the adults in the room can't do anything to help Stevie, either. None of them look like they work out on a regular basis. All they can do is wring their hands and say, "My goodness!"

The two muscleheads from Meathead, who are probably the only ones who can yank Coach Ball off Stevie, run out of the cafeteria the instant their top salesman goes ballistic.

That means there's not a single person in the cafeteria who can do anything to help Stevie or stop Coach Ball.

But wait a second.

What if we all worked together?

"E pluribus unum!" I shout, because I read it on a dollar bill. "Out of many, one!"

"Huh?" shouts everybody else in the cafeteria.

"If we all work together, we can pin Coach Ball to the mat!"

"There is no mat!" cries Gilda.

"So we'll pin him to the gross cafeteria floor!"

Gilda gives a thumbs-up. "Works for me!"

"Cowabunga!" shouts Gaynor, who's always the first to dive into anything.

"Chaaarge!" cries Pierce. "Leap into the fray! 'Cry "Havoc!" and let slip the dogs of war'!"

In a flash, 530 kids storm to the center of the room, hop on Coach Ball's back, trip him up, and wrestle him to the ground.

Mrs. Critchett, the school board president, calls the cops.

While we wait for them to arrive, Stevie yanks up on Coach Ball's pants to give him an atomic wedgie.

"It's the last wedgie of my bullying career, Jamie," he says, raising his right hand. "I promise! No more swirly whirlies, either!"

So today marks the end of two lifelong bullies, in two very different ways!

Chapter 55

LIBRARY HOURS

The following week, the library is still humming.

It's like the whole school has rediscovered
a buried treasure. Or maybe Ms. Denning just
took that treasure and polished it up a little
so it could shine. There are new book displays.
Cool collaboration stations—computer desks
where teams can work together on class projects.
A makerspace room filled with electronic bits
and LEGOs. Two chess games are taking place.
Bookworms are curled up on beanbag chairs, lost in
novels. Vincent O'Neil is in the stacks, checking out
more joke books.

Best of all, there is no more talk of turning the
library into a sweat room for the wrestling team.

In fact, Long Beach Middle School won't have a wrestling team this year. And Lars Johannsen is moving back to Minnesota with his family. His parents think the water on Long Island doesn't agree with Lars's delicate digestive tract. Thanks to the Meathead shakes, he's been spending way too much time on the toilet since they moved here.

So, we did it, folks. The library will remain the school's number one information resource center, where everybody is free to study anything and everything they want.

And there are all sorts of new classes being taught—during free periods and after school. Stuff like coding, Photoshop 101, iMovie editing, and how to bake a banana cream pie.

That one was Principal Bumgarten's idea.

That's right. The vice principal took over for Coach Ball on Friday night—right after the police arrested him for assaulting a student and taking kickbacks from a shady protein shake company. (His next move was going to be to change our school mascot from the minnow to an amino acid.)

The police towed away Coach Ball's Maserati, too. Ms. Bumgarten's vehicle is now parked in the principal's space. She drives a very sensible Prius. Her stomach is feeling much better, too. Surprise, surprise—it really helps your stress level not to have someone yelling at you all day long.

The library is so much fun now, it's totally crammed.

Ms. Denning says she might need to hire a student assistant. Since Gilda, Gaynor, Pierce, and I are all going back to shooting *Jamie Funnie* next week, Vincent O'Neil *desperately* wants Ms. Denning to pick him. He's trying to joke his way to the head of the line.

Note to self: Bring Ms. Denning some earplugs.

One week after Coach Ball was hauled out of the cafeteria in handcuffs, Uncle Frankie pops in after his lunch rush with a set of yo-yo manuals. Yep, he's going to teach an after-school class, too: You and Your Yo.

When he looks around the packed library, he's thrilled. "You did it, kiddo. You saved the library and Flora's—I mean Ms. Denning's—job."

"We *all* did," I say.

Frankie grins. "Teamwork. It's what makes the world go 'round."

"Actually," says Pierce, popping his head up over an astronomy book, "what makes Earth go 'round is conservation of angular momentum."

"Whaa?" says Uncle Frankie.

"Don't worry," I tell him. "I don't understand him very often, either."

"Guess we both need to check out a few more books, huh?"

"Totally."

After wrapping up his yo-yo class, Uncle Frankie checks his wristwatch. "You ready to roll?"

"Always."

Uncle Frankie grins. "How about Stevie and Gilda?"

"They'll meet us out front."

"Great." Uncle Frankie sets his yo-yo manuals down on a counter. "We better hit the road. We don't want to keep your new students waiting."

Oh, yeah, I forgot to mention...

I have one more class to teach.

And it's a two-hour drive north.

Chapter 56

THERE'S ALWAYS HOPE

The Hope Trust Children's Rehabilitation Center is where I lived after the car wreck that made me who I am today: an orphan in a wheelchair.

Yep. I was feeling pretty hopeless when I first arrived on its leafy campus in upstate New York. In fact, a lot of us patients called it the Hopeless Hotel. But at Hope Trust, the doctors and nurses and orderlies refused to give up on any of us, even when we'd all sort of given up on ourselves.

My doc, Dr. David Sherman, told me that "laughter is the best medicine," so he'd always bring me a couple of joke books or comedy videos from the hospital library. Every day I'd read everything I could about comedians and jokes and comedy sketches. Even when I was in a full body cast, I kept studying comedy.

I think all that laughing is what kept me alive.

Which is why Gilda, Stevie, Uncle Frankie, and I have come back. If anybody could benefit from the School of Laughs, it's these guys. Kids who are exactly where I was a few years ago. Scared. In pain. Feeling hopeless.

We set up in the hospital cafeteria.

The new Long Beach Middle School principal, Ms. Bumgarten, and *her* after-school class in the library made us the props we need for the comedy bit we're about to do. They baked us two dozen banana cream pies.

The place is packed. It's wall-to-wall wheelchairs and walkers and medical people dressed in pastel-colored scrubs. I scan the tables and all I see are tired medical workers, scared parents, and sad kids.

I see myself when I was here.

"You ready, cuz?" I ask Stevie.

He's sweating like crazy. The way I sometimes did (and still do) before a big show.

"I guess," says Stevie, sounding semiterrified (instead of his usual totally terrifying).

"Just have fun with it," coaches Gilda, our ace director.

"And make sure you make a mess!" adds Uncle Frankie with a wink.

Stevie finally smiles. "That I can do!"

Chapter 57

PI R FUNNY

Ladies and gentlemen, boys and girls," I announce. "I am Professor Jamie Grimm from the School of Laughs."

"And," says Stevie, "I am Stevie Kosgrov, Jamie's cousin and number one star student."

"Today's lesson?" I say. "The history of slapstick."

"You want me to slap you with a stick?" says Stevie. "No problem, Jamie. Bend over!"

"No can do, Stevie," I say. "If I bend over, I'll fall out of my chair. In fact, for this lesson, you should be seated, too."

"Why?"

"It'll make things easier. Trust me."

Stevie shrugs. And sits down in a chair next to me.

I turn to the crowd. "Now, I could give you guys a boring lecture about how the silent-movie greats like Laurel and Hardy, Charlie Chaplin, Harold Lloyd, and Buster Keaton all became famous comedians because they *showed* their jokes instead of *telling* them."

"*Borrrring!*" bellows Stevie.

"You're right. So instead of telling you about slapstick, I will show you."

I pick up a pie box. Open it. Pull out a banana cream pie.

And slam it into Stevie's face.

The crowd goes crazy with laughter. Yep. The classic bit still works.

"My, that was very funny," says Stevie, his face covered with whipped cream and gloppy banana goop. "I wonder if it would be funny if I did it, too!"

And he slams me in the face with a pie from the pile of boxes.

The place goes nuts.

I wipe the cream out of my eyes.

"What's everybody laughing at?" I say, pretending to be mad.

"You!" says Stevie.

"But I'm the professor! This is my class! Show some respect!"

"Okay," says Stevie. "I respect you so much, I think I'll give you more pie than anybody else!"

And he slams me again.

I'm glad we asked Ms. Bumgarten's class to bake us two dozen pies—we're gonna need 'em all! Stevie and I launch into a good old-fashioned slapstick pie fight. We even let some of the kids join in on the sloppy fun. Gilda, too. She sneaks up behind me and creams the back of my head. Slimy, cold pie crud oozes down my shirt and into my underwear.

"You ready for seconds, Stevie?" I shout.

"Hit me!"

"Oooh. Poor choice of words, cuz."

I slam him with another pie.

I'm going to need a bigger mop, too.

Pie Fight!

Stevie and I make a pretty good comedy team. Add in Gilda and we're like the Three Stooges.

More importantly, everyone in that cafeteria is having a blast. It's kind of hard to feel sorry for yourself when you feel sorrier for the guys onstage getting creamed with pies. And if Stevie and I can laugh our way through the messy humiliation of a food fight—and all the sad, painful, angry stuff that came before it—maybe our audience can do the same thing, too.

It's like Uncle Frankie says.

Be kind, because everyone you meet could be fighting a hard battle you know nothing about.

So I say…keep 'em laughing.

Because something as silly and funny as a pie to the face might make those secret battles a little easier to fight.

When we're all out of pies, Gilda comes over and kisses me. I don't think it's because she loves the taste of banana cream pie. And you know what? I don't think it'll be our last kiss, either.

"Jamie Grimm?" she says. "You funny!"

"Thanks," I tell her. "You super awesome!"

"Remember, we start filming *Jamie Funnie* in a few days," Gilda says.

I smack my forehead. "We never came up with ideas for the new episodes! I was too busy worrying about the library and Coach Ball and Ms. Denning and—"

"Are you kidding?" Gilda smiles and sweeps her hand around at the laughing kids and Stevie doing fist pumps. "If all this isn't funny enough to make your audience laugh, nothing will!"

Sticks and stones
may break your bones,
but mean names
last forever!

GET A SNEAK PEEK AT

Pottymouth
and
Stoopid

COMING JUNE 2017!

When you're Pottymouth and Stoopid, you get blamed for all sorts of stuff you didn't actually do.

Remember that disgusting lunch in the cafeteria?

The mystery meat in the mushy sauce on a bed of rice that might've been moving? The one everybody called "When You Find Out What It Is, Don't Tell Me"?

Well, somehow, that was our fault.

"Stoopid gave them

the recipe," went the rumor. "And Pottymouth told them to pour schnizzleflick all over it."

When the basketball team lost its first game, everybody blamed Michael.

"Pottymouth called the other team fluffer-knuckles. That's why we lost. He fired up the enemy with his pottymouthing!"

Not true, of course, but the truth seldom has anything to do with a good Pottymouth or Stoopid story.

For instance, did you know that I'm the one who opened the hamster cage in the fifth-grade classroom and set Scruffy free? Yeah, I didn't know it either. From what I heard, I saw the word *ham* on the cage. I thought there was a sandwich inside and I was hungry.

Then there was that disastrous field trip to the natural history museum. The trip when the whole *Tyrannosaurus rex* skeleton in the lobby toppled to the ground. They say I yanked out an anklebone so I could take it home to my dog.

I don't even have a dog, I told anybody who'd listen. Which would be nobody.

When Anna started hanging out with us, she got blamed for stuff too.

The power outage during the big vampire battle scene in the movie everybody was watching during study hall?

"Anna Britannica pulled the plug on the extension cord," proclaimed Kaya Kennecky. "She thought it was a bright orange Twizzler and tried to eat it."

And so it went. Day after day.

Pottymouth did this. Stoopid did that. Anna Britannica did everything else.

I realized that Michael and I had been Pottymouth and Stoopid for so long, most of the kids at school didn't know our real names.

That was okay, I guess.

Because we didn't want to know their names either.

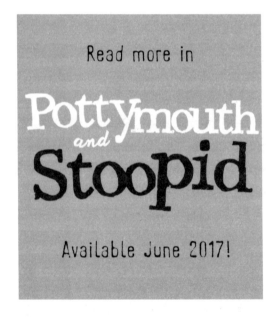

Read more in

Pottymouth and Stoopid

Available June 2017!

About the Authors

James Patterson is the internationally bestselling author of the highly praised Middle School books, *Homeroom Diaries, Kenny Wright: Superhero*, and the I Funny, Treasure Hunters, House of Robots, Confessions, Maximum Ride, Witch & Wizard and Daniel X series. James Patterson has been the most borrowed author in UK libraries for the past ten years in a row and his books have sold more than 325 million copies worldwide, making him one of the bestselling authors of all time. He lives in Florida.

Chris Grabenstein is a *New York Times* bestselling author who has collaborated with James Patterson on the I Funny, Treasure Hunters, and House of Robots series, as well as *Jacky Ha-Ha, Word of Mouse, Pottymouth and Stoopid,* and *Laugh Out Loud*. He lives in New York City.

Jomike Tejido is an author-illustrator who has illustrated more than one hundred children's books. He is based in Manila, and once got into trouble in school for passing around funny cartoons during class. He now does this for a living and shares his jokes with his seven-year-old daughter, Sophia.